PENGUIN BOOKS
ACROSS THE LINE

Nayanika Mahtani once harboured dreams of becoming a stage actor, but she followed the proverbial left side of her brain to do an MBA at IIM Bangalore and became an investment banker. A decade later, she followed her heart to live in Africa. Since then, she's been following the right side of her brain and is now an author and screenwriter. Nayanika's books include *Ambushed* and *The Gory Story of Genghis Khan (aka Don't Mess with the Mongols)*. She has also recently co-written the story and screenplay for a Hindi film based on the extraordinary life of the mathematical genius, Shakuntala Devi. Nayanika lives in London with her family, their dog, hamster and two goldfish named Sushi and Fishfinger.

ADVANCE PRAISE FOR THE BOOK

'This evocative tale of heartache buoyed by hope, travels from 1947 towards the present, tugging at our heartstrings and sweeping us along. A compelling and uplifting story that lingers long after the last page is turned'—Vidya Balan

Nayanika Mahtani

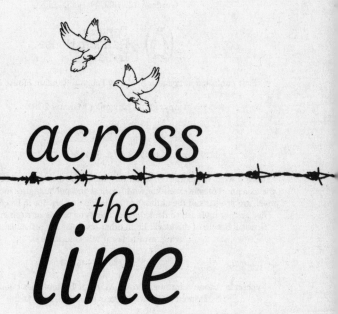

across
the
line

PENGUIN BOOKS

An imprint of Penguin Random House

PENGUIN BOOKS

USA | Canada | UK | Ireland | Australia
New Zealand | India | South Africa | China

Penguin Books is part of the Penguin Random House group of companies
whose addresses can be found at global.penguinrandomhouse.com

Published by Penguin Random House India Pvt. Ltd
7th Floor, Infinity Tower C, DLF Cyber City,
Gurgaon 122 002, Haryana, India

First published in Penguin Books by Penguin Random House India 2019

Copyright © Nayanika Mahtani 2019

All rights reserved

10 9 8 7 6 5 4 3 2 1

ISBN 9780143446033

Typeset in Adobe Garamond Pro by Manipal Technologies Limited, Manipal
Printed at Thomson Press India Ltd, New Delhi

www.penguin.co.in

In loving memory of my grandparents,
Ved and Kishori Lal Suri, and
Indra and Manohar Lal Nanda,
who lit up my world

'You—you alone will have the stars as no one else has them . . . In one of the stars I shall be living. In one of them I shall be laughing. And so it will be as if all the stars were laughing, when you look at the sky at night . . . You—only you—will have stars that can laugh.'

—Antoine de Saint-Exupéry,
The Little Prince

'There's always a story. It's all stories, really. The sun coming up every day is a story. Everything's got a story in it. Change the story, change the world.'

—Terry Pratchett,
A Hat Full of Sky

1947

'The truth isn't easily pinned to a page. In the bathtub of history the truth is harder to hold than the soap, and much more difficult to find . . .'

—*Terry Pratchett*, Sourcery

Drawing the Line

The man looked up from the maps he had been poring over. His hands were clammy, partly from the heat but mostly from the enormity of the task he had been assigned. He mopped the sweat off his brow. Then, Cyril Radcliffe picked up his pen, drew a deep breath—and a dark line.

He set the pen down. There. The deed was done. Radcliffe surveyed the map. He had carved out parts of India to form East and West Pakistan. Just as they had asked him to do. He lifted the heavy receiver of the telephone and dialled a number.

'Mountbatten speaking,' answered the viceroy of India.

'I've done what you asked, Dickie,' said Radcliffe.

'Perfect,' said Mountbatten, euphoric that this damned line had been drawn and done with. He could now head back to Britain. And go down in history as the viceroy who benevolently handed India back her freedom.

'It's far from perfe—' Radcliffe began saying.

'Not to worry, Cyril. I'm sure you've done the best you could manage, given that you had only five weeks.'

'*And* given that I knew nothing about India or cartography—and had to work with out-of-date census figures and maps with absolutely *no* expert help. As you were well aware,' Radcliffe thought to himself bitterly.

But what he heard himself say was, 'I suppose you're right, Dickie.'

Lord Louis Mountbatten barely registered his reply. He could already picture himself making headlines. Across the world. The empire's blue-eyed boy. Dressed in his spotless navy uniform. Rows of medals emblazoning his chest.

Radcliffe cleared his throat, interrupting Mountbatten's train of thought. 'Well, I believe I've completed the task I was called to do,' he said.

'Yes, yes, Cyril, and most importantly, you've served your country well.'

Radcliffe shifted uneasily in his chair. 'I'd like to return to England now, Dickie. I fear there may be violence here.'

'You can leave tomorrow, if you choose to. I'd recommend staying back to watch the whole ceremony, of course. It's going to be quite a grand affair, I'm told.'

Radcliffe could almost hear the unctuous smile slide into Mountbatten's voice.

'Just remember though, Cyril,' he continued conspiratorially, 'The line has to remain a closely guarded secret. In fact, I think it will be better if we announce the new borders a couple of days *after* we officially hand over power.'

Radcliffe clenched his jaw. It was excruciatingly infuriating dealing with Mountbatten's whimsy and utter disregard for due process. He had been picked for this infernal job of drawing the line because he was considered the most brilliant barrister in England. But Mountbatten made it almost impossible to function. Radcliffe drew a deep breath.

'Dickie, you do realize that doing that would mean that India and Pakistan will not know their borders when they get independence . . . '

'Yes, yes. But they will get to know, just a couple of days later. And then, the natives can handle their own mess.'

Radcliffe dabbed his damp forehead. 'Are you saying that our troops will not help with the relocation of people? There will be an absolute bloodbath if this isn't handled properly.'

'Our troops are going home, Cyril. The Indians have long wanted us to leave. Let the new Indian and Pakistani governments take on this challenge themselves,' said Mountbatten, darkly amused.

Radcliffe felt a dull, cramping ache grip his stomach. 'I frankly fail to see the point of this exercise. Butchering a country like a leg of lamb—it's madness!' he said through gritted teeth.

The static in the telephone line crackled. Lord Mountbatten leaned back in his chair. 'Well, there is method to the madness, Cyril. Don't quote me, but this Partition idea was Churchill's brainchild, helped along by my predecessor, Lord Wavell.'

'But why . . . what's in it for them? We're leaving anyway.'

'Aha! This is where the plot thickens,' said Mountbatten. 'You see, it's a clever ploy to protect Britain's strategic interests. Churchill felt that the creation of Pakistan would allow England much-needed control over the port of Karachi, even if we could no longer have all of India. Besides, with India and Russia's growing closeness, he reckoned that it would be useful to have a "friendly" government in Pakistan that hadn't done jail time under British rule. Stroke of genius, if you ask me.'

Radcliffe pushed his spectacles higher up the bridge of his nose, as if that might help him see things clearer. None of this made any sense to him.

'But I was told this Partition was being done because the Hindus and Muslims hated each other so much that they wanted separate countries?'

'Ah, that's just the old Divide and Rule tactic. It never fails. And frankly, it makes my job much easier.'

Radcliffe shook his head, utterly disenchanted with the whole affair.

'By the by, I've suggested we hand over power on 15 August, Cyril. It's the date that Japan surrendered to the Allies, when I was supreme allied commander. It's a lucky date for me.'

'What better reason could there be?' Radcliffe muttered under his breath.

'Sorry, didn't catch you there? Awful lot of static in the telephone connection.'

'Erm, it was nothing. I'll be in touch, Dickie.'

Radcliffe put down the receiver and slumped forward on his desk, kneading his forehead with his fingers. The ceiling fan overhead whirred slowly, helping neither the heat nor the throbbing in his head.

He looked at all the papers spread out before him. Reams and reams of paper. Survey maps and census figures about the millions who lived in the Punjab and Bengal—the two states that the line would cleave through. In a fit of rage, he swept his arm across the desk, flinging the files across the room.

As the documents lay scattered on the floor, Radcliffe's eyes fell on the papers at his feet. Staring back at him was the map of undivided India and the line he had drawn through her. As he watched, the wretched line seemed to swell up like a river of blood. A bloody river that rose off the page to engulf him. Radcliffe averted his eyes, unable to face what he'd done.

The Radcliffe Line, it would be called.

It was this line that would cause a million deaths and cause fourteen million people to become refugees. It was this line that would alter the course of history, festering like a wound that one keeps picking the scab off.

And it was this line that would cut through the heart of ten-year-old Toshi's life.

Paper Boats

12 August 1947
Rawalpindi, undivided India

If there were to be held a worldwide contest for making paper boats, Toshi Sahni would win. Hands down. It's what she did when she was bored in class. Which happened a lot. Which was probably why she was so good at it.

It wasn't just the speed of making the paper boats. It was also the little touches she would add—like chiselling chalk into the shape of oars with Papaji's razor blade, which she had secretly borrowed for the task.

Funnily enough, it was a piece of chalk that interrupted her current efforts. It hit her right in the centre of her forehead.

'Ouch!' said Toshi, looking up.

Looming large on the horizon was her geography teacher, Sharma sir, peering at her, from under a very furrowed brow.

'Toshi Sahni, why is it that you are spending your school life making paper boats instead of paying attention to our discussion on the rivers of India?'

'Er . . .' mumbled Toshi, scrunching the little boat in her fist and burying the blade into her pocket.

'Maybe she wants to ride down the Indus in that boat, sir,' offered her classmate Adil.

This caused a few giggles that only angered Sharma sir further. His forehead now crumpled into deep ravines, much like those he had been teaching the class about in the last lesson.

'Adil, is your name Toshi?' he asked.

'No, sir,' Adil replied. And then mumbled, 'Thankfully not,' to the boy sitting next to him, who ducked under his desk to laugh and stay out of Sharma sir's field of vision.

Sharma sir turned back to Toshi.

'Can you tell the class why the River Indus is important to us, Toshi?'

'Er, because our country is named after it?' Toshi offered hopefully.

'Well, yes, that's one reason . . .' Sharma sir began.

'So, if our country's name changed, would the Indus not be important any more, sir?' interjected Adil, forever on the lookout for opportunities to divert the class from whatever agenda the teacher had in mind.

'Adil Qureshi! I've had enough of your silly questions,' said Sharma sir, raising his voice and yet another piece of chalk.

He glanced at his watch as he did so. Fifteen minutes to go before the bell rang. Fifteen long minutes before he could have a cup of tea and a cigarette. He sighed and turned his attention back to his notes on the rivers of India.

Zero Hour

13 August 1947
New Delhi, undivided India

Edwina Mountbatten looked out of the imposing windows of the viceroy's palace, as she sullenly sipped her tea.

'It's going to be difficult to get used to living without all this, Dickie. I'm going to miss it.'

'Hmm. It certainly will be hard to get by in England without a home that is larger than the Palace of Versailles and has eight tennis courts, a swimming pool, billiards rooms, a nine-hole golf course, a cricket pitch, stables and kennels. Do you think we'll cope?'

Edwina sighed deeply, unmoved by her husband's attempt at humour.

Lord Mountbatten took a look at his watch. 'I'm late,' he said. 'There's a problem with the handover date that needs sorting, apparently. I'll see you at supper.'

His wife sighed again and returned her attention to the magnificent view of Raisina Hill from her window seat.

'Cheer up, darling. I've managed to get my hands on the Bob Hope film that we wanted to watch,' said Lord Mountbatten. '*My Favourite Brunette*—how does that sound?'

Edwina gave her husband a watery smile, 'That makes it all *so* much better, Dickie.'

Fifteen minutes later in a conference room nearby, the handover date was being sorted rather animatedly. A small, mousy looking official pointed to some charts that he had laid out on Mountbatten's desk.

'Sir, our pundits say that 15 August is an inauspicious date. According to the alignment of the planets, it's a very bad mahurat, sir,' he said, shaking his head in disapproval.

'Oh, for heaven's sake. That's a load of waffle!' exclaimed Mountbatten. 'We honestly can't be deciding dates based on luck or other such hocus-pocus! Please say something to help me here, Jawahar.'

Seated across him, Jawaharlal Nehru nodded wearily, 'Don't worry, Dickie. We'll work something out.'

The creases in the official's forehead seemed to sharpen, as his mind ticked. He looked around the table and hesitantly cleared his throat. 'Sir, perhaps we can time the hand over for midnight? Because, according to the English calendar, the day starts after midnight, but according to the Hindu astronomical calendar—the *panchang*—the day starts at sunrise. That way, we could perhaps mitigate the inauspicious nature of events?'

This suggestion was met with a murmur of assent from all present. The official jumped to his feet, relieved to finally have something that everyone agreed on, especially in these tediously fickle times. He was tired of the endless submissions and rejections of proposals, which merely added to his paperwork, with little being achieved. What with the Mahatma having vehemently opposed the very idea of Partition and with Mohammad Ali Jinnah and Nehru in deadlock about most issues.

'I'll start making the necessary arrangements, sir,' he said, quickly exiting the room.

As expected, Lord Mountbatten wanted to be present in both Karachi and Delhi to hand over power (and face the shutterbugs, as the world watched). But even a viceroy couldn't be in two places at the same time.

'I could transfer power to Pakistan on 14 August,' he suggested. 'And then I could fly back to Delhi to do the honours on the 15th.'

And so it was. Mountbatten flew out to Karachi on the 14th to keep up his glorious charade of largesse, as he presided over the peaceful transfer of power to Jinnah, the first governor general of Pakistan.

The viceroy then took the flight back to New Delhi.

As midnight neared, members of India's Constituent Assembly listened in silence to the chimes of the hour. A member blew a conch shell in Parliament right after, as if to summon the gods to witness a great event.

But the events that followed were far, far more ungodly than anyone had predicted.

The Referee

In the little gully outside her home, Toshi tied her dupatta securely around her waist, so it wouldn't trip her up when she ran. Then she bent down and carefully arranged stones in a pile, counting them as she went.

'Four, five, six and . . . ? Where did the seventh stone go?' she asked, looking around.

Her six-year-old brother, Tarlok, sheepishly extracted an oval, olive green quartz pebble from his pocket and held it out in his closed fist.

'Can I have this back after we finish playing?' he asked. 'It looks like a bulbul's egg, see!' He unfurled his fist with the flourish of a magician performing the grand finale of a magic trick.

Toshi sighed. 'Yes, yes—you can have the silly stone back. Why don't you collect better things instead, Loki?'

Without waiting for his answer, she turned away and placed the seventh stone on the wobbling tower, balancing it with some difficulty given the quartz's irregular shape.

'There. That's our stone tower. Do you remember how to play *pithoo*, Loki?'

Tarlok nodded vigorously, 'We have to break the stone tower with the ball.'

'Yes, but you only win if you can then rebuild it without getting hit by the ball.'

'But don't we need more people to play, Toshi di?'

'Tsk, in my version we can play with just the two of us. Do you want to play or not? Once Biji comes back, that's the end of our pithoo.'

Toshi quickly glanced over her shoulder to check if her mother was on her way back from the market. Both she and Tarlok knew that as soon as she was home, they would have to go indoors and have their customary bath before dinner.

'Let's start quickly then, Toshi di,' said Tarlok, hopping from foot to foot to warm up.

Toshi shut her left eye and aimed the ball at the pile of stones. She hit her target dead on, causing the stone tower to topple over. She whooped with joy. Tarlok ran after the ball. He scooped it up and threw it at his sister. The ball hit Toshi squarely in the back just as she was picking up the stones to rebuild the tower.

'I got you!' said Tarlok, grinning.

'Ha! You're cheating. It's just that you can pick up the ball faster because you have three thumbs. If you had two, like the rest of us, then we'd see who wins.' Toshi crossed her arms, tucking her hands under her armpits, as she usually did when things didn't go her way.

'That doesn't make any sense. I'm just better,' said Tarlok, delighted to see his sister getting riled.

'We need a referee. I'll bring Nanhi out so she can be our referee.'

'Huh? Nanhi's a doll! How can a doll be a referee?'

'Of course, she can. She speaks to me. I'll be back in a second.'

Tarlok slammed his palm against his forehead in despair at his sister's strange convictions. Toshi ran into the house to get her favourite rag doll, one that her mother had sewn for her on her fifth birthday. While he waited, Tarlok picked up the green pebble from the ground—casually tossing it high in the air and deftly catching it.

As Toshi climbed the staircase to her bedroom, she could hear the distant sound of raucous chanting. It wasn't like anything she had heard before. It seemed to be drawing closer by the minute—so much so that Toshi could feel tremors in the ground that rattled the shutters of her bedroom window.

Entering her bedroom, Toshi quickly picked up her doll and peered out of her window to see what the ruckus was about. She saw a frenzied mob approaching, brandishing long sticks as they surged forward. Now they were just a few houses away. Her gaze moved closer home. And Toshi's heart stopped.

Tarlok was nowhere to be seen.

The doll fell from her nerveless fingers on to the street below. Within minutes, Nanhi was trampled upon, mangled by the mob. Toshi watched in shock as her precious rag doll lay there torn apart, in two exquisite halves, connected by a thousand threads.

Brushing away her tears, Toshi tore down the stairs to look for her brother. Just as she was about to leave the house, her father entered and quickly bolted the door.

'Papaji—Tarlok! He's outside. We need to get him!'

'He isn't outside, Toshi. Your mother must have . . . She must have taken him to Yasmin's house upon seeing the rioters,' said Baldev. His breath was rapid, he looked deeply disturbed. 'Go to the terrace with Badi Ma and Bade Papa—I will bring Tarlok and your mother and join you.'

Toshi began to protest, but just then, her grandmother Chand emerged from the kitchen, halfway through her cooking, ladle in hand. Her grandfather Lekhraj, who was in the midst of lighting the evening diya in their prayer room, also entered the hallway, still holding the lit match.

'What is going on? Who are these people, beta?' Chand asked.

'They're from the neighbouring village, Biji,' said Baldev, hastily shutting the windows one by one. 'The borders have been announced. Rawalpindi is now in Pakistan.'

The ladle dropped from Chand's hand. 'What! But . . . but how can that be?'

'No. No, there must be some mistake,' muttered Lekhraj, almost to himself. The flame from the matchstick scorched his finger, but he barely noticed.

Baldev blew out the match and took his parents gently by their hands, herding them and Toshi up the stairs, as fast as he could manage.

'It's better if you all wait on the terrace. Hindu homes are being targeted.'

'But the rice is half-cooked—it's still on the flame,' protested Chand.

'I'll turn the gas off, Biji. You all wait upstairs please until this mob passes.'

Chand held Toshi close as they walked up the stairs, wrapping her dupatta protectively around her, as if it were a shield that would keep the mob at bay. Baldev grasped his father's arm, as he hobbled up the railing-less staircase.

'Wait here. I'll be back soon,' said Baldev, leaving them at the terrace landing.

As he turned to go, Baldev noticed their elderly neighbour, Zulaikha Gafoor, standing on her terrace, leaning over the edge of the parapet, looking down. Her face was ashen—as if she'd seen a ghost. Baldev followed her gaze. The angry band of marauders, armed with sickles, axes, sticks and spears, had stopped right outside Baldev's house. Their leader was barking incendiary orders.

'Flush out each and every *kaafir*! Don't spare a single one of these infidels.'

Zulaikha gestured urgently to Baldev to bring his family on to her terrace. 'Quickly, Baldev beta. All of you hide here. They will kill you,' she whispered hoarsely.

Zulaikha's frail frame was now the sturdiest support the Sahni family had. Baldev took one look at the barbaric frenzy of the rioters. He picked up Toshi in his arms and took a leap across the gap that separated the two terrace walls. Then he returned and helped his elderly parents make the difficult crossing, while Zulaikha extended her hand to help from the other side, each fervently hoping that they wouldn't be spotted by the mob below.

'I'll be back with Nalini and Tarlok,' Baldev whispered to them, as they sat crouched on the terrace. He took his parents' and daughter's hands in his and touched them to his eyes.

'Wait until these rioters leave, beta,' urged Lekhraj.

'It's not safe to go . . . ' protested Chand.

'Papaji! Someone's entering our house—through the kitchen door!' gasped Toshi. Peeping through the diamond-shaped holes in the parapet, she had noticed a man in the gloaming, sideling towards the rear entrance of their house.

Baldev cautiously raised his head over the edge of the parapet and saw him too. On looking closer, he realized that the man was his childhood friend, Abrar Ansari. Baldev felt a knot tighten in his stomach, as he watched Abrar quietly inch closer. Why was Abrar risking his life, approaching their house at this time? Abrar was almost at their kitchen door when someone from the mob noticed the tulsi plant in the Sahni family's courtyard—a dead giveaway of a Hindu abode.

'Look, a kaafir!' he shouted, spotting Abrar's furtive movements.

The cry ricocheted off the walls, getting the mob's attention, even amidst all the clamour.

'What's a kaafir, Badi Ma?' Toshi whispered to her grandmother. Chand didn't reply. With trembling hands, she pulled Toshi closer. From the road below, Toshi could hear Abrar's pleas.

'I'm not Hindu. I'm Muslim. Please, believe me!'

But the mob was in no mood to listen. The man who had spotted Abrar brought his axe down on Abrar's skull. The crack resonated through the air. Abrar collapsed in a bloody heap, losing consciousness. One rioter doused him in kerosene while another set him ablaze.

'Allahu Akbar!' their cries rang out, triumphant.

Chand covered Toshi's eyes with her palms, as they sat huddled on the floor. Toshi flinched at the icy touch of her grandmother's usually warm hands. She wriggled free and peered through the holes in the parapet once again.

'Abrar Chachu's burning, Papaji!' she screamed.

Instinctively, Chand clamped her palm over Toshi's mouth, afraid that they would attract the attention of the rampaging mob. Numb with shock, Baldev watched his friend's limp body burn. Still on his knees, he scrambled towards the edge of the terrace to go down to Abrar, but his mother clutched his arm.

'Don't go, beta—they will kill you too—'

She stopped mid-sentence because their collective attention was diverted by the overpowering smell of smoke and the roar of shattering window panes. They watched in disbelief as their house succumbed to the inferno that engulfed it. The fire hungrily devoured everything in its path. Toshi couldn't tear her eyes away from the wisps of red and blue flames that were licking at the familiar walls of what was once her home.

Toshi's head throbbed. Biji and Tarlok. She wanted her mother and brother. Safe from the fire and the mob. By her side. That was all Toshi could think of.

The rioters were beginning to move on, in search of their next target. Baldev was already at the far edge of Zulaikha's terrace, making his way back downstairs.

'Meet us in the attic when you return, Baldev beta,' called Zulaikha, wrapping her arms protectively around Toshi and Chand's shoulders as, still crouching, they inched towards her terrace door.

Baldev turned to look back.

'Thank you, Zulaikha Baaji.'

'You call me your elder sister, yet you thank me,' she chided, her voice thick with emotion. 'Go now, get them quickly!'

Toshi watched her father cross over to what was left of their terrace. She heard the familiar creak of the jaali terrace door as it opened. She watched him hurry down the first flight of stairs.

It was the last time ten-year-old Toshi ever saw her father.

Musaafir Khaana

17 August 1947
New Delhi, India

'Musaafir Khaana' was what their house was called. A rest house for travellers.

The name was misleading, giving the impression of a wayside inn. Rather, this was more in the way of a grand haveli, even if it was in need of some upkeep. A semicircular driveway lined by amaltas trees led to the wide verandas flanking the front door. Black, wrought-iron balustrades secured balconies that overlooked the overgrown gardens.

In the living room, Arjumand Haider was completing the embroidery on a new set of towels for her guest bathroom. Her extended family was due to come down for Eid, and she wanted everything to be shipshape and ready for them.

Her son, Javed, seemed restless—more so than usual, today.

'There's been more trouble, Ammi. Even in Aligarh. Bhaijaan also thinks it's better for us to leave. Apparently, Junaid Khan—that news reporter for the *Dawn*—has been

hacked to death. Bhaijaan says Muslim families everywhere
are being targeted and butchered. Even the children aren't
spared.'

His mother looked up from her embroidery and shook
her head. 'Javed, these are all just the vile schemes of people
who want to disrupt our country's unity. It will pass. Did
you not hear about how the Mahatma was cheered when he
visited Lucknow?'

Javed sighed. 'I don't know what to believe any more,
Ammi. Your sister and family are talking of leaving for
Karachi. Now Bhaijaan also wants to go. And Rukhsana
is due to have the baby next month. I'd rather our baby is
born in—'

His mother looked up sharply. 'Say it!' she snapped,
'You'd rather that the baby is born far away from the place
where generations of our family have lived and died. I don't
know what this world is coming to, Javed. Do what you
want. I will die here and be buried next to my husband.' She
stabbed at her embroidery angrily.

Just then, their elderly cook, Ghanshyam came running
into the house. 'Bibiji! A mob of rioters is approaching our
streets. It is not safe for you here any more. You should leave
immediately. They say the rioters are headed towards Azad
Nagar. Please come with me. My home is humble, Bibiji, but
you can hide there safely until you get a chance to leave.'

Arjumand looked up from her embroidery, ready to
launch into another tirade, but something in Ghanshyam's
eyes told her that this was not the time. She shifted her gaze
to Javed, whose forehead was lined with worry.

'Ghanshyam is right, Ammi,' he said, coming to her side. 'We need to leave. Immediately. Rukhsana!' His decibel level rose with the tide of his panic, 'Where is she?'

'It's Sunday. She's at the orphanage, as usual,' his mother replied.

'I'll go and get her. Ammi—please pack your things. We'll leave as soon as I bring Rukhsana home.' Javed rushed out of the house.

Arjumand gathered up her embroidery and walked to her room in a troubled reverie. The events of the past few months seemed absolutely senseless to her. It was as if the whole world had lost its mind. She opened her cupboard and gazed at the vast array of saris and shawls hanging there. Row upon row of silks—Kanchipurams and Banarasis, chiffons and handwoven cottons, not to mention the exquisite pashmina and shahtoosh. In a corner of the cupboard, wrapped in muslin, lay her emerald green wedding gharara, its beautiful silver zari as resplendent as it was on the day she had been wed.

Her eyes fell on her dresser, with the many photographs of her family arranged on it. Her husband as a little boy, standing with his parents, against the imposing backdrop of Musaafir Khaana. Arjumand herself, in her bridal finery with her handsome husband. The two of them dressed in Kashmiri phirans on their honeymoon in Gulmarg, chaperoned by a clutch of aunts as was the tradition, all dutifully smiling for the camera. Her parents with five-year-old Javed and all his cousins on their first-ever horse ride on the ridge in Simla. Sepia memories of little moments that had defined her world.

Arjumand sat down heavily on the edge of her bed. What could she leave behind? What could she possibly take?

An hour later, Arjumand had only managed to pack her prayer mat, the photographs on her dresser and a few clothes, when there was a knock on her bedroom door. Arjumand turned to see Ghanshyam hesitating at the threshold of her room.

'Yes, Ghanshyam? Has Javed sent you to call me?'

'No, Bibiji. I just came to say that Raghu is downstairs.'

'Oh! I haven't met him in so long. He has forgotten us now that he has got a big government job, huh?'

Raghu was Ghanshyam's son, whom Arjumand had known since he was a little boy. It was upon Arjumand's insistence that Raghu had been sent to school rather than be groomed to follow in his father's footsteps as domestic help. When Raghu completed his schooling, Arjumand had used her contacts to get him a compounder's job in a government hospital nearby.

Ghanshyam shifted awkwardly from one foot to the other, grappling for the right words, 'He's here to say that you should take refuge in the hospital for the night, Bibiji,' he said apologetically. 'He doesn't think our home is safe enough for you. He's got a taxi waiting for you outside.'

Arjumand clicked her tongue in exasperation. 'All this is not necessary, Ghanshyam. All of you are overreacting—let me speak with Javed and sort things out.'

'Javed Sahib is already at the hospital with Rukhsana Bibi, awaiting your arrival, Bibiji. Raghu spotted them near the orphanage and took them to the hospital, as the insurgents had already started making trouble. Then he came here to get you and . . .'

Ghanshyam's words evaporated as he heard distant chants of 'Har har Mahadev! Har har Mahadev!' His face grew pale and his voice took on a desperate urgency, 'Please, Bibiji. We need to be quick. Please go with Raghu. These rioters are opportunists—ransacking homes and . . . committing terrible atrocities . . . please leave, Bibiji—'

He broke off, too upset to talk. Arjumand shut her eyes and sighed heavily. 'If you say so, Ghanshyam. But I will return soon—as soon as this dark cloud lifts.'

Ghanshyam's eyes glazed over, 'I'll be waiting for that day, Bibiji.'

Arjumand reached into her cupboard and handed Ghanshyam an embroidered silk purse. 'In case I miss Raghu's wedding at the end of this month, give these ruby earrings to his wife from me. You've done more for us than family would, Ghanshyam.'

Ghanshyam quietly wiped away a tear with his sleeve. He had worked with the Haiders his whole life, just as his father had before him. Seven decades of loyalty stood steadfast. 'This . . . your having to leave like this . . . I'm so . . . so sorry, Bibiji.'

He shook his head, unable to find the words to express his deep sense of shame at what his community was inflicting upon the Haiders.

'It isn't anyone's fault, Ghanshyam. It's a madness that has possessed us all,' said Arjumand. 'Now take me away from here, before I change my mind. And make sure we are ready with the Eid preparations when I return. The whole family will descend on us in three weeks.'

As if Nothing Had Happened

18 August 1947
Rawalpindi, Pakistan

The platform was stained crimson; strewn with bloodied bodies. People heedlessly stepped over the corpses as if they were fallen leaves, whilst they madly scrambled to wangle their way on to a train. Pushing and shoving to get a foothold—anywhere. On the roof. On a window ledge. Or on the footboard, hanging precariously by the door handles of the carriages. Just as long as they were aboard a train bound for the India that lay across the line.

It was on one such train that Toshi and her grandparents were being urged to get on to by their neighbours, Zulaikha and her son, Khalid.

'Once you're across the border, you'll be safe, Chachajaan,' said Khalid to Lekhraj. 'Please don't worry, I will look out for Baldev, Nalini and Tarlok and put them on the next train as soon as I can. Things are so bad here—these people will kill you if you stay.'

Lekhraj looked at Khalid with vacant eyes. 'How do you kill someone who has died already?' he asked flatly.

Khalid swallowed hard. Fighting back her tears, Zulaikha turned to Chand, 'Do it for Toshi—please!' she said, clutching Chand's hands. 'They won't spare her life here.'

Toshi stood by Chand's side, transfixed by what she saw around her. The ten-year-old's porous gaze soaked up everything around her, especially things that adult eyes chose not to see. Like the train that had arrived a few moments earlier from India, with blood seeping out from under the carriage doors. Toshi watched wide-eyed as railway officials flung the piles of lifeless bodies that lay inside the coaches on to the platform, as casually as one might flick a piece of lint off one's coat. She felt threads of nausea rise up in her throat.

'They're getting the train ready for you,' said Zulaikha, doing her best to make this sound like one of the Sahni family's usual jaunts to Bombay or Mussoorie for the summer.

The train's whistle blew, signalling its imminent departure.

Zulaikha reached out and embraced Chand. Friends since they were newly-weds, they had spent a lifetime sharing each other's joys and sorrows. Neither had dreamt that they'd see a day like this.

As she turned to go, Chand handed Zulaikha the crescent-shaped silver key ring that she always carried. Edged with tiny silver bells, it held the keys to their house, all the storerooms and almirahs—its jingling would warn Toshi and Tarlok of their grandmother's arrival.

'Will you keep these keys please, Zulaikha?' she said. There was finality in Chand's tone, as if she knew then that she would never be able to return home. Zulaikha held her close and silently wept. The train's whistle sounded again. No further words were said. Toshi's grandparents helped her clamber up the high steps on to the train, holding her little hands tight, and with heavy, unsteady footsteps, they too climbed aboard.

As the train left the platform, something shifted in Toshi's world.

Until the day Toshi's grandmother died, she never again uttered a word about the land she grew up in; the home of her childhood; the mulberry trees she climbed with her sisters; the tube well she splashed around in with her cousins; the mohalla she played in with her friends; the temple she visited every full moon with her family; the home she got married into; the sharing of food, gossip and laughter with her neighbours; the births and deaths, thread ceremonies and marriages that were witnessed by the tulsi in her courtyard. It was as if in one swift blow, a million memories had been erased. Perhaps it was the only way she knew to deal with the numbing pain of her crushing loss. And the only way to somehow still keep carrying on.

As if nothing had happened.

Until the day he died, Toshi's grandfather would visit the railway platform every evening and sit silently on a bench.

'Who are you waiting for?' the station master would ask him.

'My family is yet to join me,' he would reply matter-of-factly. Some days he would call out 'Baldev! Nalini! Tarlok!' repeatedly, as if hoping to see them emerge from the other side of the railway tracks. Over time, the station master learnt to ignore the old man and go about his duties.

It was as if in one swift blow, time had stopped for Lekhraj. Yet, he went through the motions, unable to accept reality and hoping, deliriously, against hope that everything would return to how it was, once the dust had settled. Perhaps it was the only way he knew to deal with the numbing pain of his crushing loss. And the only way to somehow still keep carrying on.

As if nothing had happened.

As for Toshi, she learnt to navigate life without her parents. She learnt not to broach what had happened in the past with her grandparents. However, what she could *not* learn was to ever forgive herself for leaving Tarlok alone that day in the gully outside their home in Rawalpindi. So, she decided to bury her sadness deep, deep inside her little heart. Perhaps it was the only way she knew to deal with the numbing pain of her crushing loss. And the only way to somehow still keep carrying on.

As if nothing had happened.

No Man's Land

19 August 1947

Foot caravans, each several miles long, crossed each other in funereal silence as they trudged past the barbed wire fences into no man's land—the barren stretch of land that separated the newly carved Pakistan from India.

One, a caravan of Muslim men, women and children, headed to the newly formed Pakistan, carrying remnants of the life they had left behind in India in small cloth bundles. The other, of Hindus rendered homeless, headed the opposite way. Both fleeing the ferocity of the genocide that had followed the announcement of the new borders.

Not a single word was exchanged. But in those silent, wounded glances, so much was said. Of kinship. Of loss. Of becoming refugees.

By the simple drawing of a line.

'*Who are we but the stories we tell ourselves, about ourselves, and believe?*'

—*Scott Turow,* Ordinary Heroes

2008

Of Mice and Men

In a neatly scrubbed kitchen, Jai watched intently as his grandmother kneaded dough for tandoori rotis. His love for food and a general aversion to sport had lent a rotundness to him, which when combined with the scraggly beginnings of a fourteen-year-old's moustache, made him somewhat resemble a smallish walrus, albeit a very observant one especially if cooking was involved.

'How do we make tandoori rotis without a tandoor, Badi Ma?' asked Jai.

'I have a little trick for that,' said his grandmother enigmatically. 'Wash your hands. Once the dough is ready, I'll show you how to roll it out.'

'You've made me wash them thrice already,' groaned Jai.

But he was not one to argue—it sapped him of energy, and besides, he had figured that nothing much ever came of it. He began to roll up his shirtsleeves to wash his hands for the fourth time when his attention was caught by an incessant scratching sound from behind the wall, slightly to the left of the sink.

'Badi Ma, what's that sound?'

'As round as you can manage—it's tricky getting the shape of the roti right at first—but it comes with practice,' replied Badi Ma, as she expertly patted the dough, checking for its perfect consistency.

Jai peered at Badi Ma's hearing aid. Evidently, the battery had died.

The persistent noise continued from behind the wall. Jai inched towards it cautiously and gingerly put his hand against the wall. At that very moment, through a tiny crack in the plaster, something furry and brown jumped out at him.

Jai uttered a roar of fright and leapt back frantically, overturning the stainless steel urn of atta in the process. Badi Ma shrieked—more from seeing the mess than the mouse.

The mouse, which was by now covered in flour and rather unnerved by all the screaming, scurried along the kitchen counter in search of an exit point.

'Catch it, Jai!' urged Badi Ma.

'What! I'm not going anywhere near it,' said Jai, magnificently unimpressed by this ridiculous plan.

'*Uff!* I can't be chasing mice at my age, Jai. What if it jumps into the dal and bhindi next?' grumbled Badi Ma, as she hurriedly covered her pots and pans with lids.

The mouse had now slithered down the kitchen cupboards and was sitting behind the trolley of onions and potatoes, apparently having decided that this was its best strategy under the circumstances.

Badi Ma spotted the mouse and let out a blood-curdling war cry that startled Jai, causing him to leap again, this time overturning the dustbin and spilling its contents. On most days, an overturned dustbin would be a calamity that would have stopped Badi Ma in her tracks. But today, she was on a mission. Badi Ma charged at the mouse, brandishing her rolling pin.

'Just you wait—*khasma nu khane!*' threatened Badi Ma, using her choicest expletives. 'Coming into my kitchen and making such a nuisance. I'll teach you a lesson!'

As Badi Ma approached, the mouse dived into the tray of potatoes on the trolley, possibly in the hope of better camouflage. Badi Ma ruthlessly overturned the trolley to get at the mouse, but the nimble creature did a neat flip and disappeared through a tiny crack in the floorboards.

Badi Ma turned around and beamed at Jai, rolling pin in hand. 'See. I scared it away,' she said triumphantly, dusting the flour off her sari.

Just then, the door opened and Jai's parents walked in after their day's work. They took one look at the state of the kitchen and looked askance at the boy and his grandmother.

'I've just been teaching Jai how to make tandoori rotis,' said Badi Ma matter-of-factly. 'Every man should know how to cook.'

'Hmm. Looks like he put up quite a fight,' said Rajan, surveying the mess.

Jai's mother opened her mouth to say something, but the words seemed to get stuck in her throat. She gesticulated furiously towards the back of the kitchen. The whole family turned to look. The mouse had resurfaced—this time, having apparently decided to demonstrate its acrobatic skills, using the washing line across the rear veranda as a tightrope.

'Badi Ma, it's back!' cried Jai. 'You didn't scare it enough.'

'Do something, Rajan!' shrieked Arathi, paralyzed with fear.

Badi Ma picked up her trusty rolling pin once more, but the mouse did a somersault off the washing line, landed deftly on the kitchen counter, scampered to the floor and disappeared under the refrigerator.

Jai watched in grudging awe at the audacity and agility of the creature, both qualities that he secretly wished he had even an ounce of.

'We've never had mice before. Where on earth did that come from?' asked Rajan.

'From behind that wall, Papa,' said Jai.

'Behind . . . ? Walls are solid cement—mice can't live there,' said his father, poking at the plaster. It made a hollow sound. He looked quizzically at his family. Badi Ma took out her rolling pin and banged on the crack. The hollow sound echoed again.

'There seems to be some sort of cavity or recess here,' she said. 'Where's your toolkit, Rajan?'

'Do we really have to do this?' said Arathi, unwilling to deal with more commotion at the end of a long day. 'Isn't the place enough of a mess already?'

'There might be a whole family of mice living there, Arathi. It's better we address it right away,' said Rajan.

Arathi looked petrified at the very thought. Five minutes later, having used Rajan's toolkit for a closer investigation,

Badi Ma looked around victoriously. 'Just as I thought; there's a hidden compartment behind here,' she said, 'which the mice are probably merrily using as a home. My arthritis won't allow me to put my hand further . . . Rajan, can you check to see how deep it goes?'

Rajan inserted his hand into the crevice, but it was too large to slip inside. 'Yours is the only hand that will fit, Jai,' he said.

The uncomfortably recent memory of the mouse leaping out at him replayed in Jai's mind, prompting him to picture an entire battalion of mice pouncing on him. He flinched.

'Er, I'm hungry. Can we eat first?' he said, hoping to deflect the suggestion.

'Come on, Jai!' said Badi Ma.

Jai sighed and reluctantly slid his hand into the aperture and felt around. His hand touched something cold and hard. He was quite relieved that it wasn't warm and furry. He tried to tug at it, but it was too far for him to get a good grip. As he pulled out his hand, he spotted the fridge magnet that he'd brought back as a souvenir from a school trip to some boring museum or other.

Holding it with the tips of his fingers, he put his hand in the crevice again. The object clicked on to the magnet. Jai gently drew the magnet along with the object towards the opening and slowly dragged it out.

Jai's family watched as an old tin box emerged. Jai raised the rusty latch and peered in. Inside was a diary with faded, yellowing pages and a small velvet pouch. Jai looked at the diary. It was written in a language that Jai couldn't read.

'I wonder to whom this belonged,' he said, holding out the diary.

His mother came to his side and took a look at it.

'Give it to Badi Ma. She can read Urdu,' she said, squinting at the writing.

Jai handed the diary to his grandmother. Badi Ma opened the little diary and turned the pages. She looked at it for a few minutes in uncharacteristic silence. Her breath seemed uneven and her hands trembled slightly.

'What's the matter, Badi Ma?' Jai asked. 'Is this yours? Did you hide it a long time ago and forget all about it?'

Badi Ma shook her head.

'Are you all right, Badi Ma?'

'Huh? I'm fine, I'm fine,' she finally uttered, visibly troubled.

Jai looked questioningly at Badi Ma, not used to seeing his grandmother in this suddenly sombre mood.

'What's in the pouch, Jai?' asked his mother.

Jai reached into the pouch hesitantly and extracted something that looked like a brooch—a very large, ornate and dazzling one at that. It was encrusted with gemstones of every kind—diamonds, sapphires, rubies, emeralds—set in an exquisite floral design.

'Wow. Is this yours, Badi Ma?'

His grandmother shook her head, barely registering the question.

'Yours, Ma?' asked Jai, turning to his mother.

'I wish,' replied Arathi, taking a closer look at the exquisite ornament.

'So, if this isn't either of yours, whose is it and what is it?' asked Jai.

'It's a *paasa jhoomar* . . . ' said Arathi, raising the ornament to her forehead admiringly, 'It must cost a bomb—it looks positively regal.'

'Perhaps the diary has an address in it to help us locate its owner?' suggested Rajan. 'Or it may just be an old family heirloom left for us—you never know,' he grinned.

'That's right . . . I forgot you're a descendant of the Maharaja of Patiala!' retorted Arathi.

Rajan twirled an imaginary handlebar moustache in jest.

'My granddad did go to school with one of the Maharajas of Patiala—at Aitchison College in Lahore—so it could be a gift from his royal buddy.'

Arathi rolled her eyes. 'So, how many of your school friends have gifted you priceless antique jewellery, Rajan?'

'Can we have lunch now?' said Jai, interrupting this volley between his parents. 'And can we order pizza, please? This mouse has jumped in all the food here.'

'Come on, I'm sure that's not true, Jai,' said his father. 'Is it, Ma?' Rajan turned to look at his mother.

But she hadn't heard him. She just stood still, a faraway look in her eyes. She brought the diary close to her face and peered at it with her failing sight, holding it as if she was afraid of what she might be reminded of.

Almost inaudibly, she read out the date of the last entry in the diary: '17 August 1947.'

There's More to Life than Cricket

Rawalpindi, Pakistan

A loud crash announced Inaya's misjudged attempt at hitting a sixer in the tape-ball cricket tournament taking place in the street adjoining Haider Mansion. It startled Mudassar, the Haiders' elderly help, almost causing him to drop the figurine of the ballerina that he was dusting. A tennis ball covered in insulation tape had shot through the open French windows in the drawing room, bouncing off a painting over the mantelpiece and knocking over a crystal photo frame. The ball deftly made its way through the shards of glass that now covered the floor to finally disappear beneath the large leather sofa. Moments later, a breathless fifteen-year-old burst into the room.

'Sorry, sorry, Mudassar Chacha,' Inaya panted, pushing away the mop of unruly curls from her eyes. Impenitently, she crouched down and retrieved the ball. 'Please blame this on Zain. Please!'

There was the sound of footsteps and Inaya spun around.

'What are we blaming on Zain, Inaya?' asked her father, Irfan, as he strode in, followed at a more sedate pace by her grandparents. Inaya gulped and looked at them sheepishly. The trio surveyed the scene in silence. Inaya clutched the ball behind her back, hoping they wouldn't notice the smashed photo frame.

Inaya's grandmother straightened the painting that had tilted leftwards with the ball's impact. 'If you don't like your grandfather's paintings, you should just tell him so, Inaya. As I do,' said Humaira. 'Why go to all the trouble of taking potshots at them through windows?'

'But I do like Daada's paintings—that was an accident,' muttered Inaya.

Inaya's father retrieved the photograph that was on the floor. He carefully removed the fragments of glass and propped the photograph against the ballerina on the mantelpiece.

'Inaya, look at your great-grandmother—she was . . . the epitome of grace. She would be appalled by all this,' he said, gesturing at the destruction that lay before him. 'There's more to life than cricket, you know.'

From behind him, Humaira winked at Inaya. 'That's true. There's tennis. In fact, Ammi played very good tennis, isn't that right, Habib?' she asked her husband, who smiled at the fond memory of his mother.

'Oh yes. Ammi had a legendary backhand,' said Habib.

'But my point is that . . . ' Irfan began, unhappy with the turn of this conversation.

'Your point, Irfan,' interjected Habib, 'is that we shouldn't falsely blame somebody else for our own doing, isn't it?'

'No . . . Well, yes . . . What I mean to say is—' started Irfan, but then he just shook his head. He had a conference call with New York in ten minutes and he didn't have time for this.

'Let's not blame poor Zain for our mess, right Inaya?' said Habib, turning to his granddaughter. 'Now go and help Mudassar find another picture frame for my dear mother's photograph.'

As Inaya scampered out, Irfan threw up his hands in exasperation, 'You're both too soft on her,' he said. 'All she does is play cricket all day with that Zain and the other boys in the neighbourhood. Schoolwork is never a priority for her.'

'I don't remember doing much schoolwork myself,' said Habib. 'All I did was doodle and draw.'

'Yes, but your art gained acceptance, Abba. Inaya doesn't belong in that world of tape-ball cricket . . . It's a sheer waste of time.'

'Don't forget, she's been through a lot, Irfan,' said Humaira. 'The loss of her mother—that's something that hasn't been easy for any of us. Cricket is a wonderful outlet for her—let her play, beta.'

Irfan unconsciously winced at the mention of his wife Benaifer's death; a wound that was still raw although it was now eight years since the school, at which she had taught, had been ravaged by a bomb blast. Irfan's way of dealing with it had been to immerse himself entirely in his work since then, leaving little room for anyone or anything else.

'But where's Ammi? Why isn't she coming home?' Inaya had repeatedly asked Irfan. Consumed by his own grief, Irfan had no answers for his daughter.

Seeing this, his mother had stepped in. 'Your Ammi is watching over you from a star high above, my *kishmish*,' Humaira told Inaya.

With the innocence that only a child's heart possesses, Inaya had considered this explanation in puzzlement, which finally gave way to acceptance.

'I'll sleep on this side of the bed then,' she said, taking her pillow to the side that faced the window. 'Ammi says she likes to see my face when I sleep.'

Inaya curled herself into a little ball and squeezed her eyes shut. But she couldn't sleep. Not without the familiar touch of her mother's hand on her forehead, tenderly brushing away her curls. She lay awake, looking out.

Dark clouds flitted by her window. And from behind them peeped out a distant star.

'Ammi?' whispered Inaya.

Poster Girl

Rawalpindi, Pakistan

Thirty-four. Thirty-five. Thirty-six.

Inaya bounced the tape-covered ball against the wall, as she lay on her bed, sulking. She hated the fact that her father stopped her from doing the one thing she loved. The only thing that made her want to get out of bed. She threw the ball at the wall with far more force than was necessary. It shot back at her and almost got her in the eye, but she caught it just in time. Thirty-seven.

A thought flitted through Inaya's head, bringing on the faintest flicker of a smile. She reached under the mattress and pulled out a sports magazine. Turning to the centre spread, she unfolded a gigantic poster of Jhulan Goswami, the captain of the Indian women's cricket team. Inaya flicked through the magazine to Jhulan's interview and read it with rapt attention—for the fifth time.

Her mobile phone buzzed just then. Inaya was so absorbed in the article that she almost didn't hear the ring. She finally answered the call, still distracted.

'Hello?'

'Tell me you haven't seen the evening newspaper yet and that *I* am going to be the one to give you the most amazing news in the world, Inaya-*meri-jaan*-Haider!' gushed Saba, barely able to contain her excitement.

'I haven't seen it. But guess what, Saba? Jhulan Goswami also got interested in cricket after watching a women's World Cup match. Like me. And her parents were also dead against her taking up cricket. Like Abba is. And she ran away from home just like . . . '

'Just like you're planning to do, with me, your best friend in the whole wide universe, in tow?' gasped Saba wide-eyed, finishing Inaya's sentence for her and adding herself into the plot.

Inaya sighed. 'I can't just go to school and come back and do my Quran studies and homework and then do the same thing the next day and the next day and the next. I just can't . . . I can't live without my tape-ball cricket.'

'*Arreee*, that's why I'm calling you, you duffer—if you'd only let me get a word in. There is a tape-ball league tournament being organized for girls aged 16 and under— and I totally think you should go for the try-out. The selected players will be sent to London for the actual tournament. There's an article about it in the evening newspaper. Go, read it now!'

The magazine dropped from Inaya's hand. 'Are you joking with me, Saba? Why would anyone organize a tape-ball cricket tournament? Most people don't even consider it a proper game.'

'Well, there's this crazy, rich lady who apparently does. She's called Nabeel Said . . . '

'Hold on, Nabeel Said? As in, Nabeel's Kitchen, the one who owns all those cafés?'

'Mmmmhmmm . . . Apparently, her first love was cricket, but she was never allowed to play—being a girl and all . . . '

'Don't we know that story,' muttered Inaya.

'So anyway, this is what it says: "Now that Nabeel's cafés have done so well, she wants to do her bit to make cricket a game that every child in every street across the world can play. And what better way to do it than starting a tape-ball tournament. No expensive cricket balls and pads and gloves . . ."'

'There must be a catch somewhere, Saba . . . '

'Well, check out her website then. See for yourself if you don't believe me—even though I am the only person in the world who really supports your dream of meeting Jhulan Goswami on the pitch one day; apart from your Daada and Daadi of course . . . and maybe Zain. Perhaps Mudassar Chacha . . . ' rambled Saba, getting sidetracked as always.

'Of course, I believe you, Saba—it's just that nothing like this ever happens to me . . . '

'Nothing like this has ever happened to you *yet* . . . ' Saba interjected.

Inaya rose, all charged up. If this were true, things really were looking up. 'Saba Hussaini. You are the *best* friend that any girl could ask for,' Inaya declared.

'Tell me something I don't already know!' grinned Saba. 'So, the trials are next month. And there is practice happening every night until then.'

'How will I get away so much, Saba? Abba would never let me,' moaned Inaya, her happy bubble popping at the thought of her father's reaction.

'Well, Ramzan starts soon, so you can say that you're with me—and then, between *Tarawih* prayers and *sehri*, you can go and practise for a bit. I know some parks where tape-ball is being arranged with floodlights and all,' said Saba with quiet authority.

Inaya beamed, floodlit from within. 'What would I do without you, Saba?'

'Hmm. That is a very good question. One day, when I'm sitting in the pavilion at Lord's Cricket Ground in London watching you walk out to bat for Pakistan, I will tell the world that Inaya Haider would be nothing if it wasn't for me.'

Both girls burst out laughing.

'Okay, I've got to go now,' said Saba. 'Ammi is taking me to choose my new lehengas for Mahira's wedding.'

'Already? Isn't the wedding six months away?'

'Yes, but you know Ammi and her obsession with advance planning. Anyway, see you tomorrow at school.'

'Sure,' said Inaya. 'And Saba . . . '

'Yes?'

'Thank you,' said Inaya.

'You're most welcome, my dear,' said Saba, mimicking a British accent. 'I know you're headed to London, so you can save all this formality for the Brits, okay?'

Inaya smiled as she hung up. Then she jumped to her feet and reached for her laptop to google Nabeel Said.

'Nabeel's Kitchen' came up as expected, but what caught Inaya's attention was a website called 'Tapeball4All'. She eagerly clicked on the link. The first thing she spotted was the flashing ticker running across the screen: 'Calling all girls aged between 14 and 16 for trials for the Tapeball4All League Tournament for Under-16s. Selected players will be flown out to London for the tournament.'

A thrill leapt into Inaya's heart. She bounced up and down on the bed, then jumped off and did a little jig—interrupted midway by a peremptory knock on her bedroom door. Inaya quickly kicked the poster of Jhulan Goswami under her bed, shut her laptop cover and opened the door to find her father standing there.

'I bought you this, er, alarm clock, Inaya,' he said. 'So that you can wake up in time for sehri . . . you know, given that the *rozas* will be starting.'

Inaya reached out and took the clock from him. It was shaped like an old-fashioned radio.

'It was the only design the shop had left,' mumbled her father. 'Big rush for alarm clocks these days.'

'It's like the radio Ammi would listen to. I like it. Thanks, Abba.'

Her father looked at her as if he wanted to say something but wasn't sure where to begin. Their conversations had always been stilted, stopping and starting without getting anywhere on most occasions. 'So, how's your schoolwork going?' he said finally.

'It's fine, Abba,' Inaya replied, avoiding his gaze.

'You know, there are two kinds of people, Inaya,' continued her father, looking at a fixed point on the wall behind her. 'There are some who work hard in school and then for the rest of their life, they have a good time because of that hard work. And then, there are those who have too much of a good time in school and for the rest of their life, they have a hard time because of that.'

'Yes, Abba,' said Inaya mechanically, having heard this lecture so many times that she could recite it backwards and in her sleep.

'And your, er, cricket?' he asked, awkwardly, still not used to the idea of his daughter playing a sport that, to his mind, was reserved for boys or men.

Inaya was stumped. Should she say it was going well or just lie again? She decided on the safer option.

'I hardly get time for it because of all the homework, Abba.'

Her father nodded, although he didn't look entirely convinced.

'Anyway, I just wanted to, you know, give you that clock,' he said. 'Dinner will be ready soon . . . So come down.'

'Yes, Abba,' said Inaya. As soon as her father left, Inaya ducked under the bed and pulled out the poster she had kicked underneath. 'So sorry for doing that to you, Jhulan,' she whispered, as she gently smoothed out the creases. She held it admiringly, captivated by Jhulan Goswami's look of triumph on having clean bowled the batter.

Inaya looked at the posters on her walls. One was a map of the world and the other was of the planets in the solar system. Inaya carefully raised the solar system poster off the wall. From beneath it peeped out a poster of Sana Mir, captain of Pakistan's women's cricket team, hitting a mighty six. Inaya looked at it in awe and practised her own hook shot, before covering the poster of her hero with the solar system again.

Then she unpeeled the second poster, and in its place, put up the poster of Jhulan Goswami. A moment later, picturing her father's reaction to seeing her wall plastered with a cricketer, who was female *and* Indian, Inaya carefully covered it with the world map.

As she was about to turn away, Inaya's eye was drawn to where England was on the world map. She traced her finger from Pakistan to the United Kingdom. In her head, she could already hear the throb of a stadium—the resounding thud of bat against ball and the thunderous applause.

The promise of possibility sent a delicious shiver down Inaya's spine.

Recess

New Delhi, India

As soon as the school bell rang signalling recess, Jai shot out of the classroom and headed for the canteen before the bread pakoras ran out. He could already taste the spicy potatoes in the chickpea batter-coated bread, fried to golden perfection. His mouth watered and his pace quickened, but as he turned the corner of the hallway, four boys blocked his path.

'What's the rush, Jai?' drawled the leader of the pack, a thin, pallid youth called Ansh.

'It's time for tiffin, *yaar*. Check out that look on his face. It has bread pakora written all over it,' smirked Bhavin.

'Hey, can you get me a bread pakora too?' asked Chirag, thrusting his face so close that Jai could smell the fetid odour of his breath.

The fourth boy, Dev, jabbed Jai's stomach with his finger. 'There's no room here, man,' he said. 'I suggest we take some stuff out, before he puts more stuff in. What do you say, guys?'

51

Dev looked around at his cronies.

Ansh smirked. 'Go for it, Dev,' he said.

Without a moment's hesitation, Dev punched Jai hard in the stomach. Jai collapsed to the ground, whimpering in agony, too scared to shout or defend himself.

'Tsk! Big fail, once again. And since we couldn't make space for more bread pakoras in there, this will be of no use to you,' said Dev, as he bent down and extracted a fifty-rupee note from Jai's clenched fist. 'Better luck next time, fatso.'

The boys walked off, sniggering. As Jai lay doubled up on the floor of the corridor, he heard the sound of footsteps. He struggled to get to his feet before anyone else saw his humiliation. Just then someone rushed towards him. Jai instinctively flinched, fearing that Ansh and gang had returned for round two as they often did. He put up his arm to shield himself from their further blows.

Someone gently took his arm and supported him to the wall, so he could lean against it. Jai looked up to see his friend, Rustom.

'Was it them again, Jai?'

Jai's silence told Rustom that it was. 'They can't keep getting away with this, you know. I'll come with you to tell Lobo sir, if you like?'

Jai shook his head.

'Remember Harshad Kotecha from eighth grade? There's a rumour that he's leaving school because of them, but not before he tells Lobo everything. If you also tell Lobo, then maybe . . .'

'Listen, can I borrow some money from you, Rusty?' Jai interrupted. 'The bread pakoras will run out if we don't go soon.'

Rustom grinned.

'Sure. Forget going to Lobo. If there's anything that makes everything right for you, it's the canteen's bread pakoras.'

Talking in Riddles

Rawalpindi, Pakistan

As always, during Ramzan, the Haider family's alarm clocks went off before sunrise, in a symphony of wake-up calls. Bleary-eyed, Inaya sleepily groped in the dark for the snooze button on her new radio-shaped clock.

Just then, Humaira bustled in and switched on the lamp. 'Get up, my little kishmish, and eat your sehri,' she said, leaving a plate of steaming scrambled eggs, parathas, shammi kebabs, khajla and a cup of tea by her bedside. 'The sun will be up soon.'

Inaya sluggishly sat up, her eyes still shut. She reached for the teacup. Years of practice helped her find it without having to turn her head to look. She took a sip. And then she remembered something that sent her heartbeat racing. Today was the first day of her practice for the trials. She was going to need all the energy she could get.

She opened her eyes and took a big, eager bite of the kebabs and the khajla.

Inaya's school day stretched and yawned, but her mind was where the action was, miles away from her classroom. She pictured a packed cricket stadium resonating with applause as she hit a sixer that sailed over the heads of the fielders. She could hear the lilt in the commentator's voice: 'That is a fabulous, copybook shot from Inaya Haider . . .'

' . . . Inaya Haider! What do you think?'

Inaya was jolted back to reality by the jarring nasal drone of her history teacher, Mr Baig.

'About what, sir?' stuttered Inaya.

'About whether unicorns exist,' said Mr Baig, 'Obviously.' He looked around smugly, evidently pleased with himself. A few of Inaya's classmates sniggered at her confusion.

'He asked if we think history is important,' whispered Zain, from behind Inaya.

'We await your views with bated breath, Inaya,' said Mr Baig, tapping his foot.

Inaya looked around her and took a deep breath.

'Well, sir, I think that rather depends on the situation. I mean, learning about dead kings is not really my thing—but I like knowing who won which cricket match, right from the time cricket was invented . . .'

Inaya's words trailed off as she saw Mr Baig's expression go from incredulity to fury. The whole class was tittering by now.

'See me after class, Inaya. I think detention with extra history homework after school might help you change your mind about "dead kings".'

'Not today—please, sir,' said Inaya, almost in tears at the thought of missing cricket practice.

'Well, I'm letting you off this time, Inaya,' said Mr Baig, mistaking Inaya's tears for those of remorse. 'But I won't tolerate your inattentiveness in class next time. History is . . .'

Mr Baig may have waxed eloquent about the virtues of learning history at this juncture had he not been rudely interrupted by the school bell, much to Inaya's relief. She hurriedly stuffed her books into her bag and got ready to leave.

'Thanks for coming to my rescue, Zain,' she said, turning around. 'That buffoon is always intent on giving me detentions.'

Zain shrugged off her thanks. 'Saba told me you're trying out for the tape-ball league matches,' said Zain. 'I'm just trying to ensure you don't miss practice at the nets. It's this afternoon, right?'

Inaya nodded. Most of Inaya's knowledge about cricket and its finer points came from covertly watching Zain's cricket coaching sessions. In the beginning, Zain had been quite flattered by the attention, thinking that Inaya had taken a shine to him. It was only later that he discovered that she was far more interested in how he was being trained to read the ball, hold the bat, square his shoulders and never to hit across the line.

'Abba doesn't know about any of this, Zain,' said Inaya. 'Please don't say a word to your parents either. If anyone asks where I am, say you saw me going home with Saba.'

Zain hung his head back in mock exasperation. 'The reams of lies I've told for you over the years, Inaya; I'm going to burn in hell.'

'There's no guarantee of those promised virgins in *jannat* either,' grinned Inaya. 'Hell may not be that bad a deal.'

Zain shook his head at her. 'Inaya Haider, you are incorrigible.'

'Hmm. One thing is for sure, however. There isn't a chance in hell that anyone there will have a better vocabulary than you, Zain,' she chortled, seeing Zain scowl. 'Wish me luck,' she shouted over her shoulder.

'Not a chance in hell,' Zain shot back, a reluctant smile on his face.

In a makeshift cricket pitch, Inaya did warm-up stretches along with the dozen or so other girls who were also trying out for the tape-ball league.

'Will we really get to play in a league tournament if we're chosen, Inaya?' asked Fariha, breathless with both excitement and exertion.

'Yes,' Inaya grunted, between stretches. 'But we . . . only have . . . one chance . . . to impress . . . the selectors . . . We need to . . . give it all . . . we've got . . . in the next few weeks . . . '

'That's the easy bit, Inaya. But if we're selected, will we have to go to Karachi for the actual matches?'

'No, not Karachi . . . London . . . The league matches . . . are in the UK . . . ' she wheezed.

Fariha's face fell.

'I can't try out then,' she stopped halfway through a deep squat. 'I'll never be allowed to travel abroad on my own—and that too to play tape-ball.'

'I felt that way too, at first,' panted Inaya, continuing her sit-ups without missing a single beat. 'But then I thought . . . if everyone else was going to be writing my life's story, what was I even doing in that book?'

'Huh? What are you on about, Inaya?'

'All I'm saying is . . . what's the point of . . . all the breathing in and out, Fariha? Why not do something . . . that actually counts?'

Inaya sprang to her feet from her last sit-up and thumped Fariha on her back.

'I need to work on my cover drive. Are you ready to bowl?'

Inaya picked up her bat and raced on ahead, swinging her torso from side to side. Fariha took a deep breath, reached for the taped tennis ball lying next to her, spun it into the air and neatly caught it. She ran on to the field behind Inaya; the spring was back in her step.

Blue~Black Nothings

New Delhi, India

'How did you get that nasty bruise on your tummy, Jai?' asked Arathi, as Jai changed into his pyjamas for the night.

Jai hurriedly buttoned his shirt.

'It's nothing, Ma,' he muttered.

'Well, that's the biggest blue-black nothing I've ever seen,' said Arathi. She lifted his shirt and scrutinized the bruise.

'Is someone at school hurting you, Jai?' she asked, frowning. 'Is it that Muslim fellow? Rustom what's-his-name?'

'Rustom is my best friend. You really have to stop thinking that all Muslims are bad, Ma.'

Just then, Badi Ma walked into the room and began rummaging through Jai's things.

'Where could they be?' she muttered under her breath. Arathi, who was still clucking over the bruise, barely noticed her mother-in-law in the room.

'This is not about what *I* think, Jai—this is about *you*. I hope you aren't quietly putting up with people inflicting bruises on you, shoving you aro—' She suddenly noticed her mother-in-law, '—ask Badi Ma. She has had to put up with so much because of *those* people.'

Both Jai and Arathi looked at her expectantly.

'Ah, there they are,' said Badi Ma, picking up her spectacles from the dresser. 'It makes such a difference when you see the world through the right lens.' She sighed deeply and sat down on the bed beside Jai.

'I was just saying to Jai—' began Arathi.

'The Muslims suffered just as much as we did during the Partition, Arathi,' interjected Badi Ma softly. 'Sometimes, when I hear about people who had to leave India and go to Pakistan, I feel like I share something with them that perhaps not even my own family will understand.'

This was definitely not the first time that Jai's grandmother had broached this topic, but she usually left off without completing her stories.

'Why were you so saddened by that diary and pouch we found, Badi Ma?' Jai asked.

Badi Ma was quiet, as if riding some spiral of memory. Then Jai saw her shut the windows to whatever there was in her past. It was a look he knew only too well. It meant there would be no more information coming.

'Did you read that diary, Ma?' asked Arathi. 'What did it say? Any clue to whom it had belonged?'

Badi Ma hesitated for a split second. Then she fiddled with her hearing aid, as she sometimes did when she wanted to sidestep a question. 'Isn't it time for that wildlife show that Rajan and you watch every week, Arathi?'

Arathi glanced at the clock.

'You're right. Thanks, Ma—what would I do without you?' Arathi gave Jai a quick kiss on his forehead. 'Sleep tight, Jai—and remember, give as good as you get, okay?'

Jai nodded in outward agreement, knowing fully well that the last thing he could get away with was punching Ansh and gang in return. The very thought was ludicrous. They would beat him to a pulp after that. End of story.

'Do you want to tell me how you got hurt, Jai?' asked Badi Ma, as Arathi left the room.

Jai said nothing. He sat there, pulling at the dry skin around his fingernails.

'Well, I guess I should also go and change for the night,' said Badi Ma, standing up to leave.

'I know your hearing aid battery is fine, Badi Ma,' said Jai, looking up at his grandmother. 'Why didn't you want to answer Ma's question about the diary?'

Badi Ma refused to meet his eyes.

'If I tell you who punched me, will you tell me why you are sad?'

Badi Ma turned to look at him, tenderness in her gaze. 'Okay, tell me about that bruise,' she said, sitting down again on the bed beside him.

Jai quietly told his grandmother about the four boys who had been bullying him for the past few months. When he finished speaking, Badi Ma looked him straight in the eye, 'Why do you think they pick on you, Jai?'

'I don't know . . . Maybe it's because I . . . I don't like playing sports. I'm fat. I like cooking, drama—that's stuff they sneer at. They don't like me because I'm . . . not like them.'

Badi Ma let out a long breath. 'Let me tell you a little story, Jai,' she said slowly. 'There was once a little boy called Tarlok. He looked a lot like you, in fact. And like you, he was also gentle and kind. But one day, some mean-spirited people were very nasty with him.'

'What did they do, Badi Ma?' asked Jai, looking up earnestly at his grandmother.

Badi Ma looked as calm as she usually did, but beneath the surface, Jai could almost hear her thoughts flailing like trapped birds. Her eyes were fixed on the floor, but then she turned to face Jai.

'Just like those bullies did with you, they ganged up on him and attacked him for being different.' Badi Ma stopped abruptly. Her mouth felt parched. Like the words had dried up.

Jai nodded. 'Then what did he do?'

Badi Ma was quiet. Just when Jai thought she would say no more, she spoke again.

'He fought them with all his might, Jai—he was the bravest little boy there ever was.'

'Was?' Jai mumbled. 'Who was he? Where is he now, Badi Ma?'

'He is . . . was my little brother, Jai. He's no longer with us. But if he were here, I know that he would say, "Jai, don't be a pushover. Ever."'

Jai was grappling with the fact that, in all his life, Badi Ma had never mentioned her brother before. She barely spoke of her parents either, for that matter. All she said was that they had died when she was barely ten years old and that she was brought up by her grandparents.

'I didn't know you had a brother, Badi Ma. What happened to him?'

'It's a long story,' sighed Badi Ma. Jai reached for her hand.

'Please tell me the story, Badi Ma,' he pleaded.

Badi Ma looked at Jai's young eager face and gently caressed his forehead. 'It happened a long time ago. The year was 1947,' she began.

'The time of the Partition?'

Badi Ma nodded. 'Yes. It was August 17th—just a few days after India became a free country. We lived in Rawalpindi, which is now in Pakistan, as you know. Tarlok and I were playing pithoo in the little gully outside our house.'

'Pithoo? As in seven stones?' His mind boggled at the idea of his silver-haired grandmother as a little girl racing around, hitting seven stones with a ball.

Badi Ma's eyes glazed over. She could see the scene almost as if it had happened yesterday.

'And then?' prompted Jai.

Badi Ma looked lost, like a little child. She was struggling to find the will to step into the past; to venture into the dark crevices of her mind that she had not dared re-enter for a lifetime.

Jai was looking at her, in much the same way Tarlok would. Patiently waiting for her to finish whatever she was doing—whether it was piling the pithoo stones or fetching her doll to referee their game.

A tear, suppressed for decades, rolled down her cheek. Badi Ma wiped it away discreetly, hoping Jai hadn't noticed. But he had, of course. 'We don't have to speak about it, Badi Ma,' said Jai, most uncomfortable at seeing his usually resilient grandmother cry.

Badi Ma smiled weakly. 'I think it's time that we did, Jai,' she said. 'I think Tarlok would have wanted you to know about him.'

Jai nodded gravely. Badi Ma's eyes, greyed with cataract, took on a faraway look.

'Tarlok was a fearless little fellow. Not scared of anyone or anything. Even though he was four years younger than me, he was the braver of the two of us. We were playing pithoo that evening and . . . and a mob of very nasty people from a neighbouring village . . . ' Badi Ma's voice broke, as she groped to find the words and strength to continue, 'They, well, they attacked Tarlok. But he didn't give in. He fought with all his might—bravely pushing them away, even though he was only six years old, and they were armed with knives and sticks and axes . . . '

She stopped, unable to speak any more. Jai put an arm around his grandmother, hugging her tight. Although Jai's head was swimming with questions, he knew now was not the time to ask them.

'I wish I could go back and change what I did that day. How I wish I hadn't left him there alone . . . ' she broke down in stifled sobs—as if even releasing her grief fully was a luxury she couldn't allow herself.

Badi Ma's quiet tears wet her sari forming a dark patch where they fell, her shoulders heaved as she wept. Jai sat beside her in silence, wishing he knew what to say or do to make her feel better. 'I'm sure you would have helped if you could have, Badi Ma,' said Jai, finally. 'I wish I had a sister who loved me like you love your brother. He was very lucky.'

'No, Jai. Luck left his side a long time ago,' said Badi Ma, almost inaudibly. 'Every single day I wish that it was he who had lived, not I.'

Selection Day

Rawalpindi, Pakistan

Inaya's alarm clock was yet to go off, but she was wide awake. In fact, she had been awake for almost two hours because today was Selection Day. The excitement had staved off sleep, which was pretty annoying because she knew that to perform well, she needed to be well rested. There was no point trying, however, so Inaya jumped out of bed. As she brushed her teeth, she spoke to her reflection in the mirror.

'Today ish da day dat will dedermine de resht of your life, Inaya Haider,' she declared, through the foam bubbles, before rinsing. 'Okay, maybe that is overdoing the drama a bit, but still, today really matters. So, make it count.'

Rousing pep talk done with, Inaya quickly got ready and skipped down the steps, three at a time, to get herself breakfast. The sun hadn't risen. The world lay asleep—the deep silence punctuated only by the occasional birdcall. Inaya went to the kitchen, brought out the egg and milk cartons and expertly cracked two eggs into a cup of milk, making sure that only the yolks dropped in. She had read somewhere that

Jhulan Goswami also had her eggs like this. She was busily stirring the yolks into her milk, when Humaira entered the kitchen to have her sehri. She looked most alarmed at Inaya's breakfast preparations.

'Should I make you an omelette, Inaya? Why are you having raw eggs like this?'

'They're full of strength, Daadi. I need it today.'

'Ah, it's Selection Day, isn't it? Best of luck, my kishmish. May the whole world always be yours,' said Humaira, kissing Inaya on her forehead and then wrinkling her nose at the smell of the eggs in her glass.

'Abba doesn't know about this, Daadi . . . ' began Inaya, as she collected her kit to leave.

'I'll manage your Abba, don't you worry,' assured her grandmother. 'Go, play your best, Inaya.'

Inaya smiled widely, hugged her Daadi, whispered a thank you and raced out of the door.

Nabeel Said, an attractive woman in her forties, was dressed in an elegant shalwar kurta, with a *jamavar* stole wrapped around her head. She walked to the middle of the cricket pitch tossing the tape-ball high up into the air and catching it expertly, which seemed almost as incongruous a spectacle as having a llama wander into a local department store.

Nabeel stopped in the centre of the field where the three dozen or so girls had gathered for the trials of the tape-ball league. Standing at the back of the group, Inaya watched her keenly. Nabeel looked at their anxious but excited faces and smiled.

'I cannot tell you how happy it makes me to see you all here today. And even before the trials begin, I want to tell you that each and everyone one of you is a hero. Just for coming this far. Because I know the courage it takes to break through the walls we're up against.'

The girls gaped at her in unadulterated awe.

'But,' she continued, 'together, we'll tear those walls down. Bit by bit. Won't we?'

The girls looked at each other and mumbled a feeble 'yes'. 'My grandmother's old nanny goat has more enthusiasm than that, girls. Come on, let's have some *junoon* here. Won't we?'

The girls grinned and produced a resounding 'yes!'

'That's the spirit,' smiled Nabeel. 'Let's quickly go over the rules for the league tournament. The league format will be eleven-a-side, eight-overs per innings with no fielding restrictions. No bowler can bowl more than two overs. As you all know, there is no leg before wicket rule in tape-ball.'

Nabeel tossed the ball to one of the girls and cupped her hands, indicating that she should throw it back to her. As she tossed the ball to one girl after another, Nabeel kept speaking.

'A few tips, for what they're worth, from someone who has never had the chance to play but has loved the game. Can I bore you with them?' The girls nodded eagerly, unused to anyone actually bothering to help them with their tape-ball cricket, in any way whatsoever.

'Okay, so you can defend 12 an over, but 15 is better and you should aim for scoring 20,' said Nabeel. 'We all know that tape-ball cricket favours the batter given the shorter boundaries and the fact that one can't really get the ball to spin, but a tape-ball can be made to swing both conventionally and in reverse, especially as it gets older. So, I'd like to see all you bowlers work on your pace to get your yorkers right—we want them to be blindingly fast and late-swinging. But, watch out for the pitfalls. Don't let tape-ball tempt you into using a slinging action. Else, you'll be disqualified from the league.'

The girls looked at each other, nervous about the high expectations of them and overawed by the attention they were getting from this very accomplished lady, who was a celebrity in her own right.

'Some last words of advice. Those of you who get selected today are going to be up against international players—and to compete with them, peak fitness and total dedication are essential. So, either take this seriously and give it everything you have or quit right now. We cannot afford to drop this ball of opportunity.'

Just as she said that, Inaya who had been paying more attention to Nabeel's words than to the ball, fumbled and dropped the ball that Nabeel had thrown her way. Inaya's face flushed with embarrassment as she bent to pick it up. She felt like such a goof. Of all the days in the world, why did she have to drop the ball today, just when Nabeel Said had told them that it was the one thing they should *not* be doing?

Meanwhile, Nabeel was waiting for Inaya to throw the ball back to her. As was everyone else. Inaya flushed an even deeper shade of pink, sensing all eyes on her.

'And if you *do* happen to drop the ball,' continued Nabeel, with the hint of a smile, 'just pick it up and throw it again. Never stop believing—that's the most important thing.'

As Inaya tossed the ball back to Nabeel, she stole a glance at the other girls. Some of them seemed to be having second thoughts about this venture.

'Also, I forgot to mention,' said Nabeel, 'There will be a cash prize of one lakh rupees for the winning team, as the tournament is being co-sponsored by Haris Telecom. In fact, all the matches will be relayed on their cable television networks.'

The girls could barely believe their ears. This sort of support for tape-ball or for that matter, any sport for girls, was unheard of.

'So, if we get selected, will people in Pakistan be able to watch us on television?' asked Fariha.

'Yes, absolutely,' replied Nabeel.

'I can't take part, in that case. My family would disown me,' Fariha said, crestfallen.

Nabeel looked around at the group. 'Do you know what my biggest regret is?' The girls were all ears, hanging on to her every word. 'That I didn't even try—because I let fear get in the way.'

Nabeel looked pointedly at Fariha, who still looked unconvinced. 'There will always be obstacles. They can either stop us. Or challenge us to try harder,' said Nabeel. 'The choice is ours.'

Nabeel smiled at the group. 'I know that you all have it in you to succeed. Now go on, show the world what you're made of.'

Elated, the girls sprinted off to get kitted up for their game. Whether or not they were selected, they had gained something invaluable today.

Hope. And a champion to spur them on.

We've Got News

Like most days, Jai got off the bus, trudged home, unlocked the front door, dropped his satchel, kicked off his shoes and was about to head to his room when he heard voices in the living room. He walked in to find that his parents were already home, which was very odd, given what workaholics they were.

'Have you both taken the day off?' he asked.

'We've got some news for you, Jai. Come and sit here, please,' said Rajan.

Jai's heart sank. He hated things being sprung on him. Such as acrobatic mice leaping out at him in kitchens. Or bullies pouncing on him in school hallways. Or his parents flinging this 'we've got news' thing at him in living rooms.

What were they going to say? An alarming array of lurid possibilities raced wildly through his mind. Please don't let this be the announcement of a baby brother or sister. With his luck, it would turn out to be a complete nuisance. Or then, were his parents getting a divorce? Was it about that fight he had overheard after that party they had attended last week? His mother had seemed very upset that his father had complimented Mrs Arora on her sari and not noticed that she, his wife, had had a haircut. Not a trim—a proper haircut—from shoulder-length to a bob. At which, his father had gone on about how a man had no peace—no peace at all—and was constantly terrified of saying anything—anything at all. And then his mother had said that if he wanted 'peace' so much, he was most welcome to leave and go in search of it. Was this what they wanted to discuss with him?

Jai's thoughts were interrupted by the sound of his mother talking.

' . . . and so, both Papa and I thought that it would be a good idea if I went for two months . . . '

Oh God. They *are* getting a divorce, thought Jai. He could feel a knot forming in the pit of his stomach.

'I know it'll be hard for you, Jai. But Papa and Badi Ma will be here with you,' continued Arathi.

'And besides, you can go and visit Ma whenever you like,' Rajan added.

Jai looked at his parents. 'Do you *have* to get a divorce?' he asked, his voice faltering.

His parents looked at each other in bewilderment.

'Who said anything about a divorce?' exclaimed Arathi. 'Is there something I don't know, Rajan?' She clenched her jaw and her voice dropped to a menacing rumble. 'Have you been having an affair with that wretched Anjali Arora whom you can't stop paying compliments to?'

Rajan looked entirely baffled. 'Wha—where is all this even coming from? What divorce are you talking about, Jai?'

Both of them looked at Jai, trying to recall if they had ever dropped him on his head when he was a baby.

'Er . . . why is Ma going away?' Jai asked finally.

'It's for that software assignment that I've just been telling you about. It's only for two months, but it'll be a huge promotion for me at work,' said Arathi.

'Oh, okay. Where will you be going?' asked Jai.

'To London. Haven't you been listening to a word of anything I said?' replied his mother, rather exasperated. 'Anyway, as I was saying, since you have your summer holidays soon, Badi Ma, Papa and you can all come over for a short break—unless Papa prefers to stay behind and lavish compliments on Anjali Arora's wardrobe, of course.'

Rajan shook his head and smiled. 'I'm never going to hear the end of that, am I?'

'Not until you remember to notice my haircuts too.'

'So, er, coming back to the topic,' said Jai, 'when do you have to leave, Ma?'

'Well, they're working on my travel documents—so as soon as I have the papers. Oh, I'll miss you so much Jai, but we'll email each other every day until you visit, okay?'

Jai nodded happily. What he was thinking of was the restaurants that he wanted to visit in London. He had made a list when he was ten from an issue of the *BBC Good Food* magazine that his mother had brought back after one of her work trips abroad. This list had been stuck into a special scrapbook that Jai kept updating over the years. It was all part of his preparation and research for when he would open his own café one day. 'Wraps and Rolls', it would be called. He really wanted to visit Nabeel's Kitchen in London. The magazine had carried a special feature on 'hidden gems'—cafés to watch out for—and Nabeel's Kitchen was in that list. Jai had memorized almost every word the food critic had said about how expertly Nabeel Said added a contemporary twist to traditional dishes. Jai desperately wanted to try her version of haleem rolls. Just thinking about it made him smile.

'You seem so happy about the news, Jai—just like your father,' huffed Arathi. 'The least I had hoped was for someone to be a little sad that I'm going away for two whole months.'

Just then, Toshi entered the room and heard the last snatches of what Arathi had said.

'Going away for two months? Oh, don't say that, beta,' she said to Arathi. 'Are you leaving Rajan because of that fight over the foolish compliments he was paying to that silly Anjali Arora?'

'Come and sit down, Ma,' said Arathi, sighing. 'It's got nothing to do with that. It's this software assignment that I've been offered in London.'

'Arre wah, beta,' said Toshi. 'You must go—and don't worry about a thing—we're here to hold the fort. I'll keep an eye for you on my foolish son too.'

Arathi smiled and hugged her mother-in-law.

'Rajan and I are also planning to bring you and Jai there during his summer holidays, if you like, Ma. They're putting me up in a serviced apartment, and apparently, it is quite close to your favourite cricket stadium.'

'Hmm. *Waise*, I don't really care about London, but I've always wanted to visit Lord's,' said Toshi. 'To see that balcony where Kapil Dev stood, holding the World Cup trophy in 1983.'

'Gah! That was in the last millennium,' said Jai.

'Oh, but it was *so* special,' chorused his parents and grandmother.

'That Voice'

Inaya hadn't stopped talking about Nabeel Said to her grandparents or to Zain and Saba. Of course, she had to ensure that she didn't inadvertently mention Nabeel Said to her father. She had decided that it wasn't worth telling him yet—and besides, she might never need to tell him at all, because in all likelihood, she wouldn't get selected for the league tournaments anyway.

All the same, Inaya continued to sneak off to tape-ball practice before school. She had told her grandparents about it, but Irfan had been given to believe that she was going to school for extra lessons—and he was delighted with the interest she was showing in her studies.

This morning as always, she nipped into the kitchen at the crack of dawn to get herself something to eat before she left. As she reached for the light switch, her heart skipped a beat; she sensed the presence of someone else in the kitchen. It couldn't be anyone from her family. Inaya knew the clockwork-like routines of every single person in the house.

Her grandparents came downstairs at six and her father came half an hour after that to get the newspaper.

She slowly inched back towards the telephone in the hall to dial the police emergency number. Then she heard a cough that sounded familiar. Gathering her courage, Inaya peeped into the kitchen again.

Silhouetted in the dim glow of the streetlight was her grandfather, seated at the kitchen table. He seemed to be writing something. She switched on the light. Her grandfather looked up, but there wasn't even the faintest flicker of recognition in his eyes.

'Daada?' said Inaya, approaching him tentatively.

He took no notice of her and went back to scribbling away on a piece of paper. Inaya felt utterly spooked by Daada's strange behaviour. Saba had been telling her about this book she was reading in which a young boy gets possessed by an evil djinn. Had Daada been possessed by a djinn? Why wasn't he speaking?

Inaya heard soft footsteps behind her and heaved a huge sigh of relief upon seeing her grandmother walk in.

'Daadi, something's wrong with Daada! He's behaving really odd.'

Humaira didn't seem too perturbed. 'It's okay, Inaya. He sleepwalks sometimes,' she said soothingly. 'And he draws in his sleep too, occasionally.'

'What?' said Inaya, aghast that she had no idea about this. 'Daada sleepwalks? And sleep-sketches as well?'

Her grandmother nodded. 'It's nothing to be worried about, my kishmish,' she said. 'When he wakes up, he'll take his medication—and he'll be just fine. Last night, he fell asleep watching the news and forgot to take his pill. You carry on for practice—he's fine.'

Inaya didn't think Daada looked fine, but one look at the clock told her that she needed to quickly eat and head out.

'I'll spend some time with Daada when I'm back from school,' she promised, popping two slices of bread into the toaster.

'Don't mention anything to him about this morning, Inaya—he feels embarrassed about it.'

'But why should he be embarrassed, Daadi? It's not his fault that he sleepwalks. It's just a condition . . . like being seasick or something.'

'We'll talk some more when you're back. Go now, my kishmish, before your father wakes up.'

Later that evening, Inaya sat curled in the armchair beside her grandfather, as he watched the news on the television. 'Watched' was perhaps the wrong word, as he nodded off every so often, his head drooping to one side. Inaya looked at him, wondering whether he would start sleepwalking again. She hoped not. It was unsettling enough having to deal with it this morning. And even though Daadi had said it was all fine, she had used 'that voice'. The voice that she used when she spoke about things that disturbed her, but she didn't want to admit they did. Such as the fact that Inaya's mother, Benaifer, was not Muslim but Parsi.

Inaya's parents had met while attending the same college in New York. Inaya knew that Daadi had never really been happy about her parents' marriage, although she always said that she was absolutely fine with it, using 'that voice'. So, Inaya knew everything was not fine with Daada's sleepwalking either.

Much as Inaya wanted to, she didn't broach the subject with Daada, as Daadi had specifically asked her not to. Besides, he seemed to be going about his work as usual— visiting art galleries where his pieces were being exhibited and giving lectures at colleges for the arts.

Inaya might have pressed further but she was preoccupied as well. It had been a whole week since Selection Day and there had still been no news. Inaya had reconciled herself to the fact that she wasn't going to be selected. Some of the other girls had been practising for far longer than she had. Still, the effort had been worth it, even if only to meet Nabeel Said.

'Bunch of buffoons!' boomed her grandfather's voice, out of the blue.

Inaya turned to see that Daada had woken up from his power nap and was now deeply engrossed with the latest political bulletins, adding his expletive-laden commentary to the general chaos on the television screen.

Moments later, Mudassar came in with the tea trolley. Humaira liked to have her tea poured out of her silver teapot through her silver strainer into her little porcelain teacup with a spot of milk from her silver creamer. On the other hand, her husband preferred to have his tea ready-mixed, which he slurped rather noisily from a large terracotta *kullar*, to Humaira's supercilious disdain. The trolley accordingly reflected this disparity, as if half of it had been set for some visiting royalty and the other half had been assembled in a railway station's tea stall. Also, on the trolley were a cup of hot chocolate for Inaya and a plate of steaming hot samosas for the entire family.

'Ah, thank you, Mudassar,' said Habib, sitting up and reaching for his modest cup. 'What's this?' he asked, picking up a letter that was lying on the tray.

'It came in the evening post, *huzoor*,' said Mudassar.

'It's addressed to you, Inaya,' said Habib, handing her the letter.

Inaya glanced at the envelope. It was from the Tapeball4All League. She could hardly get herself to open the letter, let alone read what it said. She thrust it towards her grandfather.

'You open it and tell me what it says, Daada, please.'

'I don't open young ladies' mail,' teased her grandfather. 'God alone knows which admirer of yours has written this— penned in blood, perhaps?'

'Oh please, Daada. I really have to know.'

Habib sighed and put down his cup of tea. He picked up the letter and using his letter opener, neatly slit open the envelope. He peered at the letter, reading it carefully. He then looked enigmatically at Inaya.

'It's from the organizers of the Tapeball4All League, Inaya. They say that you were very good, but they regret to tell you . . . '

Inaya's face fell, all her hopes collapsing like a house of cards.

'. . . that you have been selected for the tournament,' continued Habib in the same morose vein, although a twinkle crept into his eyes.

It took a few seconds for Inaya to register what her grandfather had said. She stared at him in disbelief and then dashed over to take a look at the letter herself. She read it and then re-read it to make completely sure that there had been no mistake. With a whoop of joy, she hugged her grandfather and almost upset the tea trolley in her excitement.

'Oho! What's the commotion about?' said Humaira, emerging from the prayer room. One look at Inaya waving the letter in her face told her all that she needed to know. She whooped as well, causing Mudassar to hurry back into the room, to check if anyone needed first aid.

The sound of a car rolling up the driveway was like a pinprick to everyone's ballooning enthusiasm. Inaya's father was home.

'Don't you worry, Inaya,' said her grandmother. 'Don't say anything to Irfan tonight. Let me handle it,' she said with the worldly air of a woman who had handled much more than she let on to.

'Thanks, Daadi,' said Inaya, grateful that she was not to be the one to break the news to her father.

'I'll go and tell Saba—and Zain,' she said.

'Yes, tell Zain first,' said Humaira. 'The poor boy has come by thrice already asking whether you've heard back.'

'That's only because he's so competitive, Daadi. It's not because he's happy for me or anything.'

'That's not true, Inaya. He has been such a good friend to you ever since you both could barely hold a cricket bat. Of course, he'd be happy for . . . '

'Who'd be happy? And what about?' asked Irfan walking into the room just as Inaya was preparing to slink out. 'Were you leaving, Inaya? Come and sit with us all. How have your extra classes been going?'

Irfan sat down and looked pointedly at the empty seat next to him. Inaya groaned inwardly as she came over and sat down.

'They're going fine, Abba.'

'Good, good. So, whose happiness were we talking about?' repeated Irfan.

He looked around expectantly for an answer. There was a pregnant pause—until Humaira, as usual, took charge, laying the foundation of her little plan.

'We were just saying that my sister, Adeela, would be so happy if we visited her this summer in London. Habib could also finally exhibit his art there—the Aicon Gallery has been keen to have him for ages. Should we all plan to go?'

Irfan turned to his father.

'But you've never been keen on having shows in London, Abba?'

Habib slurped his tea, buying time to come up with a suitable response. He wished, as he had done a million times before, that Humaira would give him a heads-up before launching him willy-nilly into such situations.

'Well, you're right about that. But they've been awfully persistent, so I said, why not? And of course, the only reason I would tolerate staying with Humaira's wonderfully annoying sister is if we get to watch some cricket. I think Pakistan will be playing a few matches in England soon.'

Humaira harrumphed.

'There he goes again—always finding fault with my poor sister. And what about your family, huh, Habib? Each more annoying than the other, if you ask me,' she said, airily.

'Well, if you both are keen, I can start making the bookings,' said Irfan.

'Arree, what will two old pensioners do on our own there, Irfan? Habib will drive me up the wall and round the bend with his imaginary aches and pains,' said Humaira.

Habib at this point looked genuinely pained at the allegation. 'Those aches are *not* imaginary, if I may say so,' he said. 'My little toe does throb rather painfully after a bath.'

Humaira raised an eyebrow in an I-rest-my-case expression. 'We need you youngsters around, Irfan. Inaya and you must come along as well. Inaya's holidays will be starting shortly, and you haven't taken a break for God alone knows how long. One would think that the entire world rested on your shoulders.'

Irfan smiled but shook his head.

'It's going to be very difficult for me to ask for leave, Ammi. We're undergoing a restructuring, and my job is . . . well, it's not on solid ground. But I'll make the bookings for you.'

Inaya was watching this entire scenario playing out with bated breath—latching on to every syllable, as if her life depended on it.

'Do you think you can get away, Inaya?' asked Irfan. 'Don't you have your board exams coming up?'

'Tsk, her board exams are at least a year away, Irfan,' said Humaira.

'I think I can take some time off, Abba,' said Inaya, trying her best to sound nonchalant. 'I'm up to date with all my schoolwork.'

'Yes, and she has also been doing all these *extra classes* in the mornings,' interjected Habib with a straight face.

'Hmm. Okay. In that case, if everyone is keen, I'll start making the arrangements,' said Irfan. 'This should be interesting. Especially if we do well in cricket, right?'

Irfan looked at his father for validation. But someone behind him was nodding her head vigorously.

'Yes, yes! Especially if we do well in cricket!' thought Inaya, almost jumping with joy.

She blew a big kiss to Humaira behind her father's back and mouthed, 'You're the best. Thank you, Daadi.'

Humaira winked, beaming from ear to ear.

Winging It

'Jai! Hey, Jai!' shouted Rustom, as Jai walked to the bus stop after school. 'Oi, look at this.' He ran up to Jai, his eyes shining.

'What's up, Rusty?' said Jai. 'Have you won the lottery or something?'

'Just look at this,' repeated Rustom, pointing to his phone.

'New phone?'

Rustom threw up his hands in exasperation. 'Not the phone, Jai. The message—read it.'

Jai took Rustom's phone lackadaisically and read the message aloud:

'Dear Rustom Tyebji,

Your entry for the Caption This Photo Contest has been judged the winner by this year's jury. You have won a Nikon Coolpix P80 digital camera, which has been couriered to your address along with your certificate.

Sincerely,

The DigitalPix Team.'

As if to back up his claim, Rustom held up the camera and certificate for Jai to see.

'Wow, Rusty. This is brilliant. I had no idea you were into photography.'

'Well, that's the thing. I'm not,' said Rustom. 'Do you remember that photo you'd taken, of a butterfly emerging from its cocoon, for our science project?'

Jai nodded.

'Well, I kind of borrowed that one,' he said sheepishly and then rushed on to explain, his words tumbling out over each other, 'My mom was putting so much pressure on me to enter this competition, and I really couldn't be bothered to photograph stuff. I was meaning to ask you if I could use the photograph that you had taken, but then it slipped my mind. I'm really sorry, Jai. What I came to tell you is that this camera and certificate belong to you.'

Rustom handed the certificate and camera to Jai, who just stared at them blankly, trying to process what he was hearing.

'That photograph won this Nikon camera!' repeated Jai, barely able to believe it. 'But hold on, this certificate talks about some prize for "caption photography".'

Rustom thrust a copy of the photograph towards Jai. Jai read out the caption: 'Do caterpillars know that they are going to be butterflies? Or do they just wing it?'

Jai raised an appreciative eyebrow. 'Impressive stuff, Rusty. Is this caption original or did you "borrow" this as well?'

'What matters is that you are now the proud owner of a Nikon,' said Rustom, deftly evading the question.

'That doesn't sound fair—you did all the work . . .'

'Perhaps I'll keep the certificate to show my mom,' Rustom replied, retrieving the certificate from Jai. 'That's all she cares about anyway. It'll earn me some brownie points.'

'Are you sure I should keep the camera?'

Rustom nodded emphatically, 'Send me photos of your London trip. And please, not just of food, huh?'

'What can be better than food, Rusty?' countered Jai. Rustom chuckled and fell into step with his friend.

'Hey, so you're coming for the drama auditions later today, right?'

'Nah. I'm not interested in this year's play,' said Jai, trying to sound dismissive.

'What? But you're so good at drama . . .' began Rustom and then realization dawned. 'It's because of what Ansh and gang did at the last auditions, isn't it?'

Jai kept his eyes on the ground and continued walking.

'Look, I'll be there with you, as will all the others—they won't be able to try any funny business . . .'

'I told you, I'm not interested, Rusty.'

'Who aren't you interested in, lover boy?' asked a familiar voice. 'In good old Rusty?'

Jai stopped in his tracks and looked over his shoulder. Walking behind them were Ansh and his three cronies, who had just finished football practice and were on their way to the bus stop too.

'Rusty's such a handsome fellow. How can you not be interested? You'll break his heart,' said Ansh.

Dev touched Rustom's face and pretended to swoon. The foursome fell about howling with mirth. Rustom clenched his fists and would have taken a swing at them if Jai hadn't done what he did first.

'You obviously haven't received the memo, have you, Ansh?' said Jai.

Ansh was momentarily taken aback. 'What memo?'

'The memo from Mr Lobo.'

Ansh and his sidekicks looked at each other in confusion.

'The memo to our parents,' said Jai. 'About how there's going to be an anonymous Anti-Bullying Squad chosen from the senior batch. They will be Lobo's eyes and ears. And any bullying reported by them will result in expulsion.'

There was pin-drop silence.

'There was no such memo. I'm pretty sure,' said Dev finally.

'Well, why don't you go and ask Lobo if you don't believe me?' suggested Jai.

That seemed to stump Dev. Just then, a bus arrived at the stop.

'Come on, guys,' said Ansh. 'Let's not waste any more time here.'

Ansh and his cronies gathered their bruised egos and clambered on to the bus, with considerably less swagger than before.

Rustom, who had been watching intently as this whole scene played out, turned to Jai, 'I had no clue about this, Jai. When was this memo sent out?'

'There was no memo.'

Rustom's eyes popped.

'What? They'll make chutney out of us when they find out!'

'Find out from whom, Rusty? They're hardly likely to check with Lobo.'

'But what if they check with their parents about the memo?'

'That's even less likely, Rusty. They'd be opening a can of worms. What are they going to say? "Hey mom, dad. By the way, did you get a memo from Lobo that said it was wrong to bully? Just asking randomly, you know. Not that we're actually bullying anyone or anything."'

Rustom took a long, hard look at his friend.

'You are an evil genius, Jai,' he said. 'Good stuff . . . thanks!'

'Don't thank me. Thank Tarlok,' said Jai mysteriously.

'Dude, you're *so* not making sense today.'

The Unspoken Code

Inaya, Zain and Saba were perched on the sprawling branches of the huge mango tree in Inaya's garden, eating raw mangoes. Saba had brought a bowl containing a mix of salt and red chilli powder and the three of them were taking turns, dipping the mangoes in it.

'I can't believe that you're actually going, Inaya,' said Saba.

'To be honest, I can't either,' said Inaya, biting into the mango and winking involuntarily as the tangy sourness assaulted her taste buds.

'Sorry, but Curry Cruisers sounds like a really dumb name for a cricket team, even by tape-ball standards,' said Zain.

'Oh, stop being such a snobbish party pooper, Zain,' said Saba. 'How does it matter what the team is called? What's important is that *our* Inaya will be playing in an *international* league match.'

'This must be *your* lovely Nabeel Said's way of secretly marketing her restaurant, while pretending to promote sport for girls,' said Zain.

'Wow. You really are *so* much fun to hang out with, Zain. So full of positive vibes. Always seeing the good in people,' said Saba.

Zain took a mock bow, wobbling on his perch, 'Always happy to be of service.'

'What's wrong?' Saba nudged Inaya. 'Why so quiet, suddenly?'

Inaya sighed. 'I'm going to miss the two of you. I won't know anyone at all over there. Fariha was selected but her parents aren't letting her go. So, I'm the only one from Rawalpindi.'

'I'm sure this league of yours will have lots of interesting spice girls from all over Pakistan,' said Zain. 'The Biryani Blasters, the Kofta Challengers . . . '

'Your jokes are *so* pathetic, Zain,' said Saba.

'So, what are the European teams called?' continued Zain. 'The Fish and Chippers?'

He found this so funny that he almost fell off the tree laughing. Saba shook her head and rolled her eyes.

'Uff . . . Just ignore him, Inaya.'

'Inaya Haider, you don't have to pay any attention to me, but do pay attention to all the cricketing tips you've picked up over the years from me . . . ' began Zain.

' . . . from your cricket coaching sessions, you mean,' interrupted Inaya.

'Well, at least those sessions were of use to one of us,' grinned Zain. 'Now go, smash it out of the ballpark. Show the world what Pindi is capable of.'

Zain held out his fist and both Inaya and Saba bumped fists with him.

'I still think Curry Cruisers is a seriously crappy name,' said Zain.

Saba and Inaya looked at each other and then, as if by some unspoken code, they simultaneously reached out, plucked the mangoes nearest to them and took aim at Zain.

Mind the Gap

The train journey from London's Heathrow airport to Paddington was fairly short, but it felt interminable to Inaya. Because *no one* spoke. The silence was deafening, especially after the cacophony of voices, laughter and general mayhem back home. Here, everyone studiously avoided each other's eyes and buried their noses in their books or newspapers.

Inaya sat beside her grandmother; her grandfather sat in the seat across the aisle, clearing his throat at regular intervals, the sound of which resonated throughout the hushed compartment.

'Does Adeela know we're coming today?' Habib asked his wife, leaning across the aisle between them.

'Yes, of course she does,' Humaira replied.

'I hope she's remembered to prepare some hot lunch for us, unlike the last time, when she fed us those frozen leftovers that broke my tooth and fractured my jaw.'

'How you exaggerate, Habib!' chided Humaira, while Inaya giggled. 'And while we're here, please don't make life difficult for my sister. Please just adjust. Adeela is vegan now, so please don't demand lamb curries and such.'

'Your delightful sister breathes fire and cracks walnuts with her bare hands. What choice does one have but to adjust?' said Habib.

The gentleman sitting beside him looked up from his newspaper. 'I feel your pain. I'm originally from Karachi, and I couldn't help but overhear,' he said, by way of explanation for gatecrashing this family conversation. 'Just in case you're looking for a good curry place, there's a lovely little one right by Paddington station. Nabeel's Kitchen, it's called.'

'Much appreciated, thank you. I think I will be in dire need of some such alternatives to save my remaining teeth,' said Habib.

Humaira harrumphed loudly, indicating that she had had enough of this topic and she didn't need random strangers to now start weighing in on this public takedown of her sister. Almost fifty years of marriage had taught Habib to interpret these harrumphs. He held his peace for the rest of the journey.

Meanwhile, Inaya's mind continued to flit between the excitement of playing her first ever tape-ball league match and the trepidation of what if it all went horribly wrong. She unconsciously began to drum her foot against the seat in front of her to release her pent-up nervousness.

Jai looked through the viewfinder of the camera that Rusty had given him, in the hope of getting a decent shot of the

London skyline, but all he could see was a grey blur, as the Heathrow Express shot past the scenery. Sighing, he put the camera away and turned his attention to his grandmother seated beside him.

'Why didn't Ma come to the airport to fetch us, Badi Ma?'

'Arathi's at work, Jai,' explained Toshi patiently. 'She offered to take the day off, but I told her we would manage. It's just a straightforward train ride to Paddington, and once we've left our bags at her apartment, she said she would meet us for lunch.'

'Okay. Where will we eat lunch?'

'She mentioned some place—it's very close to the station.'

Just then, a girl sitting behind Jai started to drum her foot against the seat rather annoyingly. Jai wished he had it in him to turn around and ask her to stop. But that would mean confrontation, and that was the last thing Jai wanted in this very quiet train, with everyone listening. He glanced back to see if he could discreetly catch her eye and politely request her to refrain from kicking his seat. As he did so, she caught him looking at her.

'Do you have a problem?' she asked, sharply.

Jai's ears turned red and he quickly turned away without mentioning to her that, yes, he did have a problem. That of her kicking his seat. And then behaving like *he* was the problem.

What a pesky girl, he thought to himself.

What a weird specimen, thought Inaya to herself.

Dragon Breath

Adeela Noorani stood by the window of her maisonette in Marylebone, waiting for her sister and her family to arrive.

'Oh, there she is, Humaira,' said Habib, as their taxi pulled into the driveway. As an aside to Inaya, he whispered, 'Can you see the window glass fogging up with her fiery dragon breath?'

Inaya tried to suppress her laughter, which then resulted in some fitful snorting. Humaira, displaying dignified disdain, paid no heed to any of this. She busied herself instead, with straining to catch a glimpse of her beloved younger sister.

Even an hour later, the two sisters' joyous reunion was still in full swing.

'Remember the time we played truant and snuck out from school to have *falooda* at Gawalmandi, Humaira Aapa?' asked Adeela. This seemed to spark some long-lost memory that both sisters were completely consumed by. An avalanche of anecdotal download ensued with both talking over each other in their excitement.

'I think we may have to sneak off to get some lunch,' muttered Habib to Inaya, cupping his hand over his mouth. 'What say you?'

Inaya nodded, grinning. Habib stood up and patted his tummy. 'The airline food doesn't seem to have suited me and I foolishly forgot to pack my antacids,' he announced.

'Tsk, I told you a million times to check that you have packed all your medicines, Habib . . . ' began his wife.

'I could look to see if I have some around, although I have turned to alternative medicine mostly. Would you like to try some of my natural remedies?' offered Adeela. 'Some crushed asafoetida . . . '

'Just say hing, Adeela,' interjected Humaira. 'Since when do we call it asafoetida?'

'Er, don't worry,' said Habib quickly, 'I'll just go down to the chemist around the corner and pick up something. Inaya, would you like to come for a little walk?'

'Leave the poor child with us,' said Adeela. 'She's had a long journey.'

'It's, er, fine, Adeela Khaala,' said Inaya. 'I'll go with Daada.'

'Come back soon. I've made some kale and courgette patties for lunch,' Adeela called after them; words that seemed to propel Habib and Inaya out of the door even faster.

Nabeel's Kitchen

Fifteen minutes later, Habib and Inaya arrived at Nabeel's Kitchen. There seemed to be a long queue to get a table.

'Should we go elsewhere, Daada?' said Inaya. 'It's going to take us ages here and it's not like we can't eat this food back home.'

'It's going to be the same everywhere, Inaya. Let's just wait for our turn.'

Inaya sighed and glanced out of the window, watching passers-by to pass her time.

Meanwhile, Jai and Toshi were walking towards the café where Arathi was to meet them.

'Oh, there it is—Nabeel's Kitchen,' said Jai, quickening his step as he neared it. He had wanted to eat here for ages— which was why Arathi had decided it would be the first place she would take them to for a meal.

As Jai walked past the café's window, he suddenly heard a loud shriek. He looked up to see flailing arms, and attached to them was a familiar body, which launched itself at Jai and enveloped him in a bear hug.

'I've missed you so much, my Jai,' said Arathi, as she covered her son's face with loving kisses.

'Er, hi Ma,' said Jai, mortified by this public display of affection and desperately trying to extricate himself from the maternal smother. His mother, meanwhile, seemed wholly oblivious to his plight.

Luckily for him, Arathi spotted Toshi walk up just then. She let go of Jai and bent down to touch her mother-in-law's feet. 'How are you, Ma? Was the flight okay?'

'The flight was very comfortable, beta—' Toshi was interrupted by a loud sneeze from Jai.

'Are you cold, Jai? Why didn't you pack a jacket? The weather here can be very temperamental,' scolded Arathi. She whipped her stole off and wrapped it around him, ignoring his protests.

Swathed in a floral lilac stole, Jai glanced up and caught sight of someone standing inside the café, watching him through the bay window. He had seen her before somewhere.

'It couldn't be—oh no, it is—that Pesky Girl from the train. Great. Just what I needed,' he thought in dismay, quickly disentangling himself from the stole.

'I really don't need this, Ma. I'm quite hot, actually.'

His mother had moved on to other interrogations, still ruffling his hair and being overly exuberant in general.

'Was it difficult lugging the suitcases on to the train? Did you find the house easily? Did you get a SIM card at the airport? You've lost so much weight, Jai!'

'No. Yes. Hmm, yes . . . er . . . ' he said, unable to keep pace with the battery of questions.

'I can't tell you how happy I am to see you both,' said Arathi, looking like she might relapse into another bout of public humiliation for him, in full view of the Pesky Girl.

'Same,' said Jai, almost running into the café, so that his mother couldn't latch on to him again, especially while Pesky Girl was probably still watching.

The bad news was that there was a long queue to get a table. *And* standing in front of them in the queue was Miss Pesky Girl.

'Should we just go somewhere else?' asked Toshi.

The thought of getting away from the Pesky Girl was tempting, but the epicure in Jai trumped that notion.

'The line is moving really quickly, Badi Ma,' Jai replied. 'And once you try their haleem rolls, believe me, the wait will be worth it.'

Toshi and Arathi shook their heads in resignation.

Another fifteen minutes passed, and finally, it was Habib and Inaya who were at the top of the queue. The waitress came over to Habib.

'How many of you?' she asked.

'Two, please,' Habib replied.

'Okay, you'll have to wait I'm afraid; we've only got a table for five.'

'My knees won't hold up any longer with all this standing,' said Toshi, leaning on Arathi for support.

Arathi thought for a moment and gently tapped Habib on the shoulder.

'I'm sorry, but I couldn't help overhearing the waitress, sir. Would you mind if we shared your table? We're three of us.'

'Not at all,' said Habib, rather relieved that they could get to eat sooner.

As they sat around the large table, Jai painstakingly avoided looking at Inaya. Instead, he diligently studied the menu.

'Are you ready with your order?' asked the waitress.

'Should I order for us?' offered Jai, before anyone else could respond.

'Perhaps we should allow them to order first given that they were ahead of us,' said Toshi.

Habib smiled at Jai, 'Go ahead,' he said. 'We've barely even read the menu yet.'

Jai nodded happily and launched into placing his order.

'Could we please have four of your signature haleem rolls, two tandoori fish tartare, two raan chops . . . '

'We should have ordered first, Daada,' whispered Inaya. 'I don't think there'll be anything left for us at this rate.'

' . . . two Hyderabadi dals, two nihari tokris, twelve roomali rotis and three mint raitas,' continued Jai undeterred.

'Certainly,' said the waitress turning to leave.

Habib called after her, 'Er, excuse me, could we place our order too?'

'Oh, sorry,' said the waitress, wondering if these five guests had been kept starved for ages and set free just this afternoon.

'What would you like?' she asked with a forced smile.

'Everything that they just said,' said Habib.

'But Daada, that's far too much . . . ' began Inaya.

'Don't worry, we'll doggy bag what we can't eat. From the sound of your Adeela Khaala's menu plans, we're going to need alternative arrangements to survive.'

Arathi shifted uneasily in her seat. The people she was sharing a table with had family members with very Muslim sounding names.

'So, are you from India?' she asked breezily.

'No. We're from Pakistan actually,' replied Habib.

There was a charged silence as Arathi absorbed this. It was bad enough having to sit at the same table with Muslims, but to have to do so with Muslims from Pakistan was, to her mind, beyond speakable.

In this unspeakable state of mind, she gathered up her handbag and stood up, as if she were about to make a speech to which she had forgotten the words.

Jai, whose eyes were trained on the kitchen doors, was suddenly struck by the fact that his mother was standing up at their table, for no apparent reason. 'Are you all right, Ma?'

'Yes. No. No, I don't feel very well, actually. I think we should leave,' said Arathi.

'But . . . but . . . our food . . . ' spluttered Jai.

'They can pack our food and have it delivered to our apartment,' said Toshi, realizing that Arathi was not going to stay. Knowing Arathi, Toshi had expected something like this, although she had hoped that she would be more sensible about it.

'I don't think they do home delivery here . . . ' began Jai, sounding almost heartbroken at the prospect of missing out on this meal.

'Well, then why don't you stay and bring it with you, Jai?' said Toshi. 'I'll go on home with Arathi.'

Arathi turned on her heel and left abruptly, stopping only to pay their bill and letting the waitress know that they would like their order to be packed for takeaway instead. Toshi followed. Jai looked around sheepishly at Inaya and Habib, who had been silent spectators to this drama.

'She wasn't feeling well,' Jai repeated, for want of anything else to say.

'Perhaps she's allergic to us,' said Habib with a smile. Inaya raised her eyebrows and snickered. Jai squirmed, praying that the food would arrive soon, so he could flee this uncomfortable scene.

'So, are you from India?' Habib asked conversationally.

Jai nodded.

'We crushed you in the Asia Cup,' piped up Inaya.

'Sorry, what?' said Jai, completely disconnected from any news related to sport.

'Your bowlers were weeping by the end of the tournament,' she continued.

Habib gave her a stern look to stop, but Inaya was on a roll.

'They need to eat more protein,' she said. 'Perhaps you should parcel some legs of raan and send it to your bowlers.'

Jai bristled but couldn't think of any suitably crushing comeback—especially as he was clueless about cricket. Thankfully, the waitress arrived with the packets of food shortly after.

Jai hastily collected them and made his way to the exit, hoping he would never have to see that nasty, smug piece of work again.

Sumo Wrestling

As Inaya and Habib entered Adeela's home, they could hear the raised voices of Humaira and her sister, entrenched in intense argument in the kitchen.

'It has barely been a few hours and they're already going at it hammer and tongs,' sighed Habib. 'It's a good thing that you and I got ourselves some food and fresh air.'

Inaya chuckled. She couldn't help marvelling at how her usually dignified grandmother quickly regressed into a squabbling ten-year-old whenever she was with her sister.

'Well, you would have attended the wedding if you had cared enough,' Humaira snapped at Adeela. 'It's not as if your *only* sister's *only* son gets married every day.'

'I can't believe that you're holding a grudge about something that happened seventeen years ago, Humaira Aapa,' Adeela retorted. 'And it wasn't like you were over the moon about that wedding, if I remember right. You disliked Benaifer right from the start—and only because the poor thing wasn't Muslim.'

'I did *not* dislike her. I was absolutely fine about them getting married,' retorted Humaira, at which Habib raised an incredulous eyebrow.

'Did you also not like my mother, Daada?' asked Inaya, as she followed Habib into the living room.

'Benaifer was like a daughter to me, Inaya,' replied Habib gently. 'You are so much like her. Although she did smash fewer photo frames,' he added, smiling.

Inaya pretended to be most offended and then broke into a wide grin.

'By the way, Inaya,' said Habib, 'Don't you think you were a little harsh with that poor boy at lunch?'

'No. Of course not, Daada,' Inaya replied breezily. 'Have you forgotten that *they* were the ones who left the table because we were Pakistani? *That's* harsh, if you ask me. And besides, I was just stating facts about their bowlers.'

'Hmm. Last I checked, you couldn't get enough of a certain Indian bowler named Jhulan,' said Habib.

Inaya's cheeks flushed.

'Yes, but that boy was very annoying, Daada . . . '

'You barely know him, Inaya. He seemed harmless enough.'

'You don't know that, Daada. He was on the same Heathrow Express train as us, and he was being all weird, so I had to put him in his place.'

Habib shook his head in resignation. The voices from the next room were growing shriller by the minute. Habib switched on the television in an attempt to drown them out.

'You know, Inaya, women are marvellous creatures—one of the greatest creations of the Almighty,' said Habib. 'But I have to admit that I'm possibly more grateful to the creator of the television.'

In the background, the voices of his wife and sister-in-law rose to a crescendo, but Habib blissfully tuned into the rather more subdued sumo wrestling tournament in Osaka.

War of the Roses

Since their arrival in London, Inaya had attended four warm-up games at the cricket nets in Regent's Park with the rest of the Curry Cruisers squad, and although she had been apprehensive at first, the side had bonded surprisingly well.

Today was another warm-up game for the Curry Cruisers, and since the sun was shining brightly, Humaira and Adeela decided to accompany Habib and Inaya to the practice grounds. As they walked through the park, Adeela provided a running tour guide commentary.

'And these are called Queen Mary's Gardens. Look at those beautiful roses, Humaira Aapa.'

'Pah! We have better roses in Rawalpindi,' scoffed Humaira.

'Oho, of course!' said Adeela. 'How can anything here be better than Rawalpindi?'

'You are basically a *gaddaar*, a turncoat,' retorted her sister. 'Nothing in the country of your birth is good enough for you any more, is it?'

'Well, I'm not defined by where I was born,' said Adeela pointedly. 'I'm happy anywhere on this beautiful planet of ours.'

'All these newfangled ideas of yours will get you nowhere, Adeela,' said Humaira. 'This . . . vegan thing and doing yoga and belonging to the planet—all this will only leave you without any true identity.'

'Uff, just listen to yourself, Humaira Aapa. Are you making *any* sense? Tell me, does your identity begin and end with belonging to the country that you happened to be born in?' demanded Adeela. 'To me, that seems like such a limited way of experiencing the world.'

Humaira decided not to dignify her sister's biting remark with a response, so she just upped her walking pace instead, channelling all her fury into her feet. Meanwhile, Inaya and Habib were in a quandary as to whether they should catch up with Humaira or stay in step with Adeela.

'Could I please join you for practice to escape this?' whispered Habib to Inaya, who muffled a chuckle.

'What time will your practice be over, Inaya?' asked Adeela. 'I've booked us a table for lunch at Nabeel's Kitchen . . .'

'Oh yay! Their haleem rolls were so good that day! They were totally worth the wait!' blurted Inaya.

'When did you try their haleem rolls?' asked Adeela.

'Er . . .' said Inaya, frantically scrambling for something to say.

'It was just a rushed lunch that we had the other day,' said Habib, gallantly coming to her rescue.

'Yes, it was so rushed that we had to share a table with those annoying people,' added Inaya.

Habib desperately signalled with his eyes at Inaya to simply stop talking. But it was too late. By now, Humaira was intrigued as well.

'How come I don't know about this wonderful lunch that you had, Habib?' she asked with a plastic smile. 'And who are these people that you lunched with?'

'It wasn't anyone you know, Daadi—just some random people from India who had also arrived in London the same day as us,' said Inaya.

Habib groaned inwardly, bracing himself for the inquisition that was sure to follow.

'One moment, one moment,' interjected Adeela, sounding peeved. 'Bhaijaan, you told me that you had an upset tummy—and then you went and ate at Nabeel's Kitchen? After I slaved the entire morning preparing those kale and courgette patties for you!'

Habib cringed at the thought of the almost unpalatable patty that he had been forced into trying on his return to Adeela's apartment.

'It wasn't planned,' he said. 'We were just walking past the café . . . '

Humaira and Adeela harrumphed in unison.

'Of all the people in London, could you only find Indians to share a table with, Habib?' sneered Humaira.

'Oh, come on, Humaira . . . ' began Habib.

'On this front, I'm with Bhaijaan,' cut in Adeela. 'You can't generalize about people based on where they live.'

'Naturally *you* would say that, Adeela, now that you consider yourself "British" and have abandoned all your pride in being Pakistani,' Humaira shot back.

'Can we please just enjoy the walk and not start that again?' sighed Habib.

The foursome walked in silence for a bit.

'We've reached your practice grounds, Inaya,' announced Adeela abruptly. 'Enjoy yourself. All you have to contend with is some balls hurtling at you. At least you don't have anyone tearing you down.'

Humaira chose to ignore this oblique gibe. 'Go and play your best, my kishmish,' she said.

Inaya gave them a quick hug and scooted off. She needed to put all these squabbles aside and focus. The tape-ball league tournament's first match was tomorrow. It was a knockout round, so if her team didn't perform, that would be the end of the road for them.

Too Much to Digest

Back in Arathi's cosy apartment, Toshi, Arathi and Jai were playing Scrabble. Jai picked up the letter 'Y' and placed it on the board, completing his word.

'Oh, come on, Jai. There is no such word as *Fy!*' said Arathi, turning to her mother-in-law to back her up.

'This is pure and simple cheating,' declared Toshi emphatically, taking Arathi's side.

'You always say I'm cheating when you're losing, Badi Ma! And by the way, it *is* a valid Scrabble word,' said Jai. 'It means "to digest". Look here if you don't believe me.' He held Arathi's iPad aloft triumphantly.

'You youngsters assume that everything you see on the internet is the gospel truth,' scoffed Toshi.

'Who else can we ask, Badi Ma? The web has all the answers,' teased Jai.

'Hmm. That reminds me, there's something I wanted to ask you, Arathi,' said Toshi. 'What is so wrong about sharing a table with Pakistanis?'

Jai squirmed, thinking about the uncomfortable scene that had transpired in Nabeel's Kitchen. Arathi looked at her mother-in-law in disbelief.

'What is right about it, Ma?' she countered. 'Have you forgotten all the wars we've had with them and all the times they've attacked our country? So many of our soldiers have died because of them.'

Toshi looked pained, as if someone had punched her in the gut. 'Our soldiers dying. Their soldiers dying. All this hate. Where will it all end? Especially if we can't even sit at the same table and talk anymore,' she said sadly.

'What is there to talk about with them, Ma? We have nothing in common with them—and never will,' said Arathi.

'Actually, beta,' said Toshi gently, 'I probably have more in common with people from Pakistan than say, with you. Many Pakistanis and north Indians share the same history: our language, cuisine, ancestry, poetry . . . '

'And I'm just this South Indian who will never understand that, right?' interjected Arathi, with a brittle laugh.

'That's not what I meant. All I'm saying is that we *do* have a lot in common with them. Our families have lived side by side for centuries.'

'But do these Pakistanis feel the same way about their relations with Indians, Ma? That is the question you should be asking. Maybe you're living in an idealistic bubble . . . '

'Should we carry on playing?' asked Jai, keen as ever to avoid conflict of any sort.

Toshi nodded, distractedly.

'It's your turn, Badi Ma. You need to get yourself some more letters,' said Jai, offering his grandmother the bag of alphabet tiles. 'And Badi Ma, please don't make a word on that one spot on the board because that is where my next word would fit. Really well.'

'I will make a word wherever my letters fit, Jai,' said Toshi loftily.

'Argh! I had forgotten how competitive you are, Badi Ma,' groaned Jai. 'Anyway, I do have a backup word.'

'I hope it's a real word this time, Jai. I cannot "fy" any more of your strangely obscure words,' said Arathi.

Jai grinned, relieved that the conversation had veered away from Pesky Girl and her Pakistani family. Besides, she was the last person he wanted to be reminded of.

Alphonso Season

There was very little conversation at Adeela's dinner table. Adeela was still seething at her sister's remarks. Predictably, Humaira had refused to apologize. Habib was looking rather frayed from trying to convince Humaira to take the high road and be the bigger person.

Inaya played with the peas on her plate, pretending they were balls, batting them away with her knife. One such pea, which had been struck rather well, neatly bounced off Adeela's cheek.

'Oh, stop it!' exclaimed Adeela, instinctively turning to Humaira, in a throwback to their mealtime tiffs from their childhood.

'Stop what?' asked Humaira, icily.

Adeela immediately realized that the pea had come from Inaya's plate, but Adeela wasn't going to admit that to her sister, of course. She clenched her jaw. 'Stop questioning my loyalty to my country,' she snapped, deciding to use this opportunity to air her resentment.

'I was merely observing that you have perhaps forgotten the land of your birth,' said Humaira.

'In that case, you should be embracing those Indians whom you hate so much—because if I am not mistaken you were born in India, Humaira Aapa,' countered Adeela.

An uncomfortable silence ensued, until Inaya cleared her throat and said, 'Tomorrow is my first match.' No one responded to this sally, preoccupied as they were with the rather tense slanging match between the siblings.

'Does anyone want any more asparagus?' asked Inaya, in a further attempt at steering the conversation to safer ground.

'I'll have some please, Inaya,' said Adeela, a tinge of smugness in her voice.

Grateful that at least someone other than her was speaking again, Inaya passed the dish of asparagus to Adeela, wrinkling her nose as it passed beneath it. If there was anything she considered worse than these arguments and the uncomfortable silences that followed, it was Adeela Khaala's cooking.

'Mangoes are in season,' announced Adeela, slicing through the silence. 'Inaya, will you go to the kitchen and get some for us please?'

Inaya rose quickly, grateful for this heaven-sent respite from all the awkwardness that had descended into the proceedings.

'Should I help?' offered Habib, just as keen to make his escape from the war zone.

'They're mangoes not mountains, Habib,' snapped Humaira. 'I think she will manage without your help.'

Inaya returned with half a dozen luscious mangoes.

'D'you know, when we were growing up, Inaya,' said Adeela, as she cut them and handed them around, 'Our father would get these mangoes for us, all the way from Bombay—'

Humaira, who was halfway through biting into a slice, spat it out. 'Are these Alphonso mangoes? What's wrong with you, Adeela? Why couldn't you buy our own Pakistani chaunsa mangoes?'

Adeela shook her head wistfully, 'You'd fight me over these mangoes when we were little, Humaira Aapa. What has happened to you? Just listen to yourself—do trees and fruit also have to be Indian or Pakistani?'

Humaira pushed her chair back and flounced out of the room in a huff. Adeela looked at Habib and Inaya quizzically. 'You can leave these mangoes too, if you like,' she said. 'I'll buy the chaunsa for you tomorrow.'

'It's against my religion to say no to any mango,' said Habib, taking a big, slurping bite. Inaya grinned and followed suit.

Later that night, after everyone had gone to bed, Inaya decided to sneak downstairs for a slice of the chocolate cake that Habib had secretly bought for them. She knew it wasn't a good idea to eat cake in the middle of the night before a match, but eating only vegan food was taking its toll on Inaya. She felt like a car running on an empty fuel tank, with a sadly sputtering engine.

When Inaya tiptoed into the kitchen, she saw someone standing by the gas stove. She squinted in the semi-darkness to get a better look—just then, the person turned around. In the feeble light of the gas flame, a pair of glasses glinted and Inaya recognized the silhouette. It was her grandfather. Was he sleepwalking again? Why was he near the stove? Why was he wearing his spectacles if he was asleep? Should she wake him?

Inaya flipped on the switch for the kitchen lights, 'Daada?'

There was no response. She looked at her grandfather's face. His eyes were wide open, but he didn't seem to be aware of her presence. When she drew closer, she noticed that his spectacles were fogged up—and then realized with a shock that he was holding a saucepan filled to the brim with boiling water. She quickly took the pan from him and switched off the gas flame.

'Daada, are you okay?' Habib looked at her and then reached into the pocket of his dressing gown and patted around.

'It's not there,' he said, almost to himself.

'What's not there, Daada?'

'My ro—'

But before he could finish his sentence, Humaira entered the room.

'There you are, Habib!' she said. 'I woke up and your side of the bed was empty.' It was then that Humaira noticed what Inaya was holding. She swiftly took the pan of boiling water from Inaya and emptied it into the sink.

'He does that sometimes. He tries to make tea—I've told him time and again to use the electric kettle,' said Humaira. 'He forgot his medication again, Inaya. Don't worry—go back to bed. Everything is just fine.'

It was 'that voice' again. Everything was *far* from fine.

'That boiling water was about to fall on Daada's feet, Daadi . . . '

'It looks that way, but it never happens,' said Humaira dismissively. 'You have an important match tomorrow, my kishmish. Go, go and rest now.'

Inaya reluctantly left the room, tumultuous thoughts crashing through her head, making her even forget about her craving for cake.

What was going on with Daada? And why was Daadi brushing everything aside as if it was so trivial?

Glorious Uncertainties

The stadium, if you could call it that, was the cricket field of the Paddington Recreation Ground. A large billboard announced: 'Tapeball4All League Tournament, sponsored by Nabeel's Kitchen'. Inaya sat with the rest of her Curry Cruisers teammates, chewing at her stubby fingers as she awaited her turn to bat.

'And tape-ball cricket is even more gloriously uncertain than regular cricket is!' declared the commentator who seemed either to have had too much coffee, or was generally an overexcitable sort. 'Eleven-a-side, 8 overs per innings and no fielding restrictions—really sets the scene for some fast-paced entertainment. And so, in this game of glorious uncertainties, let's see if the Curry Cruisers from Asia—comprising players from India, Pakistan and Bangladesh—can save the day. The Chippy Champs team from Europe—comprising players from the UK and Ireland—have batted first and raised an impressive score of 141 from 8 overs. That is an absolutely brilliant score in this Under 16s tournament. Will the Curry Cruisers be able to beat that total?'

The skipper of the Chippy Champs side, Simone Donnelly, was in fine form. When it was her turn to bat, she had smashed almost every Curry Cruisers bowler all over the park—and was now getting her bowlers to keep the run rate of the Curry Cruisers well in check.

Inaya was star-struck as she watched Simone, who was England's biggest female star of tape-ball. Simone, a tall strapping girl, had grown up in Birmingham playing tape-ball cricket with a bunch of children of Pakistani origin in her neighbourhood. Twenty an over was a routine achievement for her—earning her a following not only in England but in Pakistan and Dubai as well.

The Curry Cruisers had a mammoth 142-run target facing them. Their skipper Shaheen along with the other opener, got off to a very respectable start, scoring 34 runs in the first 2 overs. But then Shaheen fell victim to a superb delivery. In the next 3 overs, the next pair put on a valuable 51-run partnership, but soon after, they were both out to successive balls.

This brought Inaya Haider and Lubna Ahsan in to bat. Inaya tapped her foot nervously as she looked at the scoreboard. Three wickets down and they were only at 85. They had to score 57 in the remaining 3 overs in order to win. It was a hugely ambitious ask. Lubna was the more experienced player, but Inaya had kept the scoreboard ticking too—and in the next 2 overs, they managed to rack up a commendable 29 runs.

The last over arrived. The Curry Cruisers needed 28 to win off 6 balls. Inaya was on strike. Judith Jones, who had an outstanding record in the death overs, was brought in to bowl. The first ball of the over was a bouncer. It went high over Inaya's shoulder, sailed over the outstretched gloves of the wicketkeeper and bounced to the boundary for 4 byes. The umpire called it a wide. Inaya's heart was racing, even as she thanked her lucky stars for those much-needed runs and the extra ball.

Six balls, 23 runs needed.

Judith came up to deliver the next ball.

' . . . the Curry Cruisers will really need to pull off a miracle here,' said the commentator. 'I'd say there isn't much left in the game now . . . '

Inaya flicked it on the leg side for a 4.

'Oh, that's a surprisingly lovely shot there,' effused the commentator, in a sudden change of tone. 'Haider is managing to keep her nerve even under pressure.'

Five balls, 19 runs needed.

Inaya looked around the field, mentally mapping the placement of the fielders. She tried to smash the next ball for 4 runs through a gap in the field, but it caught the edge of her bat and flew high, towards the boundary.

'Oh, that looks like it will be caught!' said the commentator, his voice going an octave higher with every word he spoke, 'And it is!'

Inaya looked crestfallen. But seconds later, the commentator was on the air, all energized again.

'A bit of a wobble there, has the fielder lost her balance? Oops. It does look like her foot has crossed the boundary rope. Well, well, well. What can I say? The match is back on.

Inaya Haider is not out and the last delivery will now count for 6 runs.'

Inaya felt a surge of relief course through her. She took a deep breath. She must not waste this precious second chance she'd got. Now the Curry Cruisers needed 13 runs off 4 balls. Inaya was on strike. She managed to edge the ball into a gap in the fielding. Inaya and Lubna raced furiously, scoring 2 runs. The fielder threw the ball back to the bowler's end, but the bowler fumbled, giving the Curry Cruisers an extra run for the misfield. And bringing Lubna Ahsan on strike.

Ten runs needed and 3 balls to go.

The next ball almost clean bowled Lubna, skimming her bat and skidding just out of the reach of the wicketkeeper. Lubna was already tearing down the pitch for a single—and then decided to come back for a second. There was no second run in that—it was a hugely risky decision, but Lubna was more than halfway down the pitch by now. Inaya figured that if she didn't run, the fielder would throw the ball to the wicketkeeper, who was waiting to whip off the bails, and Lubna would be run out. Inaya decided to go for the run. Seeing her attempt this impossible run, the fielder scooped up the ball and threw it at the non-striker's end. Inaya flung herself and her outstretched bat on to the crease. The ball hit the wickets dead on, knocking the bails off. The Chippy Champs team went up in a synchronized 'Howzaaat?'

Inaya held her breath, waiting for the verdict. Seconds later, a cheer went up amongst the Chippy Champs players. Inaya didn't even bother looking at the umpire for his decision and started walking off the pitch. She had blown her chance.

This was the end of the road for her. Lubna looked absolutely crushed as Inaya walked past her.

'I'm sorry about that, Inaya—' she began.

Inaya shrugged it off and walked on ahead. Then she turned around and came back to Lubna.

'On a pitch like this, Judith tends to bowl a slow ball followed by a yorker in her death overs. Watch out for that.'

Lubna listened with her head cocked to a side and nodded ever so slightly.

The new batter, Dayita, was in and the Curry Cruisers now needed 9 off the last 2 balls to win. Skipper Simone signalled to her fielders to go towards the boundary—the only way the Curry Cruisers could make 9 runs off 2 balls was with at least one 6.

Judith took a longer time than usual for her run-up. Lubna was watching the ball with singular focus. Everyone was expecting Judith's famous yorker, but this ball was far slower. As it dipped and moved away, Lubna timed it perfectly, hitting it into the stands for 6 runs. Dayita met her in the middle of the wicket and fist-bumped her.

'That was brilliant, Lubna,' she said. 'We're almost there.'

But Lubna was not even listening. She was in the zone, watching Judith and Simone, as they discussed the field settings and how the last ball should be bowled. Lubna took a look around the field to see where the fielders were. She took it all in and returned her focus to watching the ball. As soon as it left Judith's hands, Lubna knew it was a yorker. She stepped back into her crease, turned the yorker into a half-volley and got under it, hitting it with a satisfying meat-of-the-bat thud. The ball sped to the boundary for a thumping 4.

Within moments, the entire Curry Cruisers team was on the field. Lubna came charging across the pitch, bent down and lifted Inaya up. Both girls collapsed on the ground, laughing.

'We did it, Inaya! We won—can you even believe it?'

'*You* did it, Lubna,' said Inaya. 'And no, I can't believe any of this—'

'Hey, girls,' said a voice behind them.

Inaya looked up to see Simone Donnelly, the skipper of the Chippy Champs.

'Oh, hi Simone,' said Inaya, rather taken aback.

Lubna jumped to her feet.

'Hi Simone.'

Simone smiled and extended her hand to Inaya, who was still sitting on the ground. Inaya took her hand and Simone helped her up to her feet.

'That was a great win—well played, girls,' she said. 'And by the way, your team spirit is tops, Inaya. Looking forward to seeing lots more of you both.'

'Thanks,' mumbled Inaya and Lubna, quite overcome.

'By the way, you probably know this, but you're absolutely brilliant, Simone,' said Lubna. 'I'm a bit of a fangirl,' she added, beaming brightly.

'Oh, I think you both have me as a fan now,' said Simone. She smiled and ran back to her teammates. Inaya and Lubna watched her go, in silence. Then Lubna plucked a blade of grass from the ground and held it up to the sky.

'I swear, by this blade of grass, that I will remember this day for the rest of my life,' she proclaimed.

'I have to say—you're *quite* the drama queen, Lubna,' said Inaya, trying to keep the excitement out of her voice. 'What's the fuss about? This is just like any other day.'

'You're right,' said Lubna. 'Except that we've just defeated a brilliant side. On their home ground. In our debut match. And Simone Donnelly just said that *she's* our fan.'

Both girls looked at each other and let out unbridled squeals of joy.

Stalkers

Inaya walked out of the Paddington Recreation Ground with Lubna, chatting away nineteen to the dozen. Even though she hadn't shone in her performance as much as she had hoped to, she was elated that her team had won the match.

'So, where in Pakistan are you from, Lubna?'

'I'm from Bangladesh, actually.'

Inaya stopped dead in her tracks.

'Seriously? Your name is so Pakistani—and you even look like, well, one of us,' she said, taking a closer look at Lubna.

'Yeah—it's hard to tell,' grinned Lubna. 'I mistook some of the Indian girls on our team to be from Bangladesh too. Have you ever been to Bangladesh, by the way?'

'Nope. But isn't Bangladesh close to where Jhulan Goswami is from?'

'Pretty close. Just across the border. You like her, huh?'

Inaya nodded.

'I too think she's amazing,' said Lubna. 'In fact, my grandmother originally comes from the same town as her family does—Chakdaha in West Bengal.'

'What! How awesome is that? Why would anyone leave the town where Jhulan comes from?'

'I know, right? I asked them the same question—they said the Partition happened,' Lubna shrugged.

As they waited at a zebra crossing, Inaya noticed a familiar face bobbing up and down in the crowd of people approaching them. Inaya grabbed Lubna's arm and made her do an about-turn.

'Come with me,' she said. 'It's lunchtime—and I've just seen someone who has a good nose for food. Let's just follow him.'

'What? You're crazy, Inaya.'

'Trust me. This will be fun,' said Inaya, with a wicked grin.

And so, unbeknownst to Jai, he was being stalked by the twosome. This time though, he wasn't headed to eat. It was his mother's birthday the next week and he was out looking for a gift for her. He boarded a bus headed for Oxford Street, oblivious to the fact that both Inaya and Lubna had also hopped on to the same bus. When he got off, so did they.

As he drifted along Oxford Street with the throng of other tourists, Jai kicked himself for not having bought his mother something in India with Rusty's help—like he always did. If there was anything Jai hated, it was shopping. He hated making decisions, especially those that had to do with buying things, and it was so much worse when he had to choose on someone else's behalf. The very thought of entering any of these shops and being approached by an overzealous salesperson gave him cold feet. Just as he was on the verge of giving up and turning back, he spotted The Body Shop. He remembered having seen some of their products on his mother's dressing table. Perhaps he could just get her something from here.

Five paces behind him, Inaya watched, rather nonplussed. This was an unexpected detour—certainly not what she had expected.

'You said your friend was some sort of restaurant expert?' whispered Lubna, as they entered the shop as well.

'I wouldn't call him that!' Inaya whispered back. 'But he has a knack for ordering the right dishes.'

'So, what should we eat here, Inaya?' said Lubna. 'Delicious mango body butter?'

Inaya burst out laughing. On hearing her laughter ring out, Jai, who was trying to make sense of the papaya face mask, looked around, swamped in dread.

'No, no, please don't let it be her,' thought Jai in desperation. But it was. That Pesky Girl. Again.

Inaya grinned widely at him.

'I'd really recommend that face mask actually,' she said. 'Papaya is great for a glowing complexion and its strong aroma masks all other odours—so you can actually go without bathing for weeks.'

Lubna started to chuckle. The tips of Jai's ears started to turn a shade of scarlet.

'It's not for me,' he bridled.

'Oh right. How silly of me. Were you buying it for someone special?' asked Inaya, loading the question with innuendo.

'No—I mean, yes,' said Jai.

At this point, Lubna's chuckles became hysterical and high-pitched. Jai glared at her. As if one pesky girl wasn't bad enough, now there were two.

'By the way, meet my friend, Lubna,' said Inaya.

'Hi,' said Lubna.

Jai mumbled an awkward hello.

'It's sweet that you're getting something for a special someone,' said Lubna, winking at Inaya.

'I'm getting late,' said Jai, returning the papaya face mask to the shelf. 'I need to go.'

'Er, before you leave, could you recommend where we could have lunch nearby?' asked Inaya.

'Tomoe Sushi is supposed to have amazing salmon nigiri according to *BBC Good Food* magazine,' said Jai, almost automatically, before exiting the shop as fast as he could.

Lubna turned to Inaya.

'Hmm. So, you like him, huh? Not a bad choice, Inaya— he seems the thoughtful, romantic sort—spending time choosing gifts and all.'

'*Like him*? You must be joking, Lubna! The only thing halfway decent about him is his knowledge of food.'

'You're so wicked, Inaya,' snickered Lubna. 'Okay, I'm starving now. Where's that sushi place of his? All this stalking had better be worth it.'

Empty-handed

'Didn't you like anything at all, Jai?' asked Toshi. 'I thought you would come back with a gift.'

Jai was still hopping mad after his encounter.

'I *had* selected something, Badi Ma, but then . . . '

'But then, what, Jai?'

'But then that Pesky Girl showed up, and she was insinuating stupid stuff and going on about masking body odour, blah, blah, blah, so I just left the shop. I should have told her off! But instead, I told her about the sushi place.'

Toshi was looking at Jai, wholly baffled, 'Which girl? What body odour? What sushi?'

'That Pakistani girl, Badi Ma. Ma was right about Pakistanis. They are just bad news. Especially the girls.'

'Do you mean that girl, who was accompanied by her grandfather, with whom we had to share a table?'

'Yes, yes, that one. I feel like she's following me everywhere. Wherever I look, she's there—laughing that annoying hyena laugh of hers.'

'Tsk, you shouldn't let anyone put you off your plans, Jai.'

Arathi came in just then, dropping her bag on to the settee and subsiding into the cushions after a hard day at work.

'Hello family! So, what are the devious schemes currently being hatched by grandmother and grandson?' she asked cheerfully.

'Er, nothing, Ma,' said Jai.

'Tomorrow's agenda—that's what we were planning,' volunteered Toshi. 'As it's your day off, should we visit Lord's and then the Tower of London? I have always wanted to pay good money to see our very own Kohinoor diamond, which was so considerately confiscated from us to be securely stored in a tower for all tourists to admire.'

Arathi laughed.

'Are you plotting a diamond heist to retrieve the Kohinoor and restore it to its rightful place in India, Ma?'

'Well, my arthritis has been playing up, so that may not be possible,' said Toshi. 'But Jai, this is now your life's mission—to reclaim the Kohinoor as our national heritage. Do not return empty-handed, is that understood?'

Jai nodded distractedly. He was concerned with more immediate missions for the moment. Such as how to give a fitting reply to Pesky Girl, should he see her again—which, with his luck, he was bound to do.

The Bridge

Inaya whistled as she waited outside Adeela's home, having rung the doorbell four times.

Then it dawned on her that her grandparents and Adeela Khaala had gone visiting a cousin of theirs and had left a spare key under the mat for her.

Inaya strolled into the house and kicked off her shoes, before she guiltily realized that she should stow them away tidily in the shoe cupboard to avoid getting another lecture. Finally, she plonked herself down on the sofa.

It still hadn't sunk in that she had qualified for the next round of the league. But now, she knew without a doubt that no matter what happened, whether she made it any further or not, she was going to give everything she had to tape-ball cricket. Nothing else made her as happy.

She had an overwhelming urge to tell everyone about this win. Especially Abba. She missed him—whether or not she admitted it to herself. More than anything else, she wanted to hear the pride in his voice when she gave him the news. However, deep down, she knew that this wouldn't be the case. He thought so little of her cricket.

How she wished Ammi was alive. Somehow, with Abba, there was always a yawning chasm that neither of them could ford, however badly they both wanted to. Inaya decided to try and bridge that gulf today. She reached for the phone, and then remembered that he would still be at work. Perhaps she should wait until he got home. She sat back down.

But then, on an impulse, Inaya got up again and went to look for her father's work telephone number in her grandmother's diary. As she rifled through the large brown moleskin diary, some papers fell out. Inaya picked them up and was about to return them to the diary, when she caught a glimpse of something on the pages.

They were sketches and they looked like they had been drawn by a small child. Inaya held them up, bemused, wondering why her Daadi had saved these in her diary. They weren't even pleasant to look at—the images looked chaotic, with many huddled figures drawn in a circular scribble, all dark and gloom. And strangely, each of the pictures had a jagged line running across it—as if the picture had been crossed out after having been drawn.

Inaya put them away and went back to looking for her father's number. When she found it, Inaya took a deep breath and dialled the number from the London phone that Adeela Khaala had given them.

'Hello,' Irfan's deep, familiar voice came through.

'Abba, it's me.'

'Is everything all right, Inaya? Are Daada and Daadi okay?' There was concern in Irfan's tone.

'They're very well, Abba. I wanted to tell you that our team won the league match today.'

There was silence at the other end.

'Abba? Are you angry with me for taking part? I'm sorry, Abba, I didn't want to hide this from you—I really wanted to share—'

'Daadi mentioned that you were playing in some games there, Inaya. I'm glad that you won and that it's all over now. I hope you'll be back soon.'

That was it? Was that all he had to say? There was no point in trying to reach out to him. It was always the same dead end. Inaya suddenly wanted to hang up. Her breath felt short and sharp.

'Hello? Inaya, are you there?'

'Yes, Abba, we'll be back next week,' she replied curtly.

'That's good, Inaya,' said Irfan. 'It seems unlikely that I'll be able to join you in London. My work won't allow me to get away . . . as I explained to your Daadi too. I need to go now, I have a meeting in five minutes.'

Inaya hung up and sat on her grandmother's bed, knees drawn up, her head cradled in her arms. So much for trying to make a connection and establishing a rapport. If anything, she felt they were even further apart than before.

The High Road

The morning dawned bright, fluffy white clouds pegged to blue skies as far as the eye could see. Arathi came into Jai's room and drew aside the curtains. Jai squinted as the sunlight pierced through his groggy daze.

'Rise and shine!' said Arathi, annoyingly bright-eyed and bushy-tailed. 'I'm off for a meeting, Jai, and then I'll meet Badi Ma and you for lunch. You choose where to eat—as long as it isn't exorbitantly priced. But before that, take Badi Ma out for a walk or something.'

'Not another walk, Ma,' groaned Jai. 'Badi Ma is arthritic. So much walking isn't good for her.'

'Nice try, Jai,' said his mother. 'Now stop being such a lazy lump. I'll see you at lunch. Didn't you say you had two more restaurants you wanted to visit before we leave? You're going to bankrupt me at this rate.'

'I've saved up some money, Ma. So, this can be my treat, since it's your birthday soon.'

Arathi beamed and gave Jai one of her bear hugs that left him gasping for breath.

'All grown up, huh, Jai? Buying me lunch already? I'm not quite ready to have my baby boy grow up though. I still want that little boy who was terrified of giraffes.'

'Er, bye Ma—I'll see you at lunch.'

Arathi smiled and left the room, blowing him a kiss, which he pretended not to notice. Jai found all this demonstration of affection most unnecessary but was never quite sure how to tell his mother to stop without hurting her feelings.

As he bathed and got dressed, the thought of choosing a lunch venue cheered him up considerably. But before that, he had to subject himself to yet another walk. He had come to the conclusion that this city required way too much walking. After this London holiday, he didn't want to go for another walk for a year or two.

'Jai? Are you ready?' called his grandmother.

'I'm coming, Badi Ma,' sighed Jai.

Jai slipped on his sweatshirt and joined Toshi at the dining table for breakfast.

'I was thinking that we could go to that recreation ground nearby for a walk today. What do you think?' asked Toshi, as they sat down to a breakfast of cereal and milk.

'How's your arthritis, Badi Ma? Aren't your joints hurting at all?' Jai asked hopefully.

Toshi gave him a knowing look. 'I'm deeply touched by your concern, Jai,' she said with a twinkle in her eye.

✠

As Adeela loaded the dishwasher after breakfast, she glanced at her sister, who seemed a little preoccupied.

'Is everything all right, Humaira Aapa?'

'Huh? Yes . . . yes, everything is fine.'

'Where is Bhaijaan? Did he not want to have breakfast this morning?'

'He had a cup of tea and left with Inaya. She has some practice games today.'

'Inaya mentioned something about him sleepwalking again last night?'

Humaira sighed deeply. 'It's something that we just have to live with. I don't think that will ever leave us.'

'It's been so many years. Why don't you seek some help while you're here, Aapa? There's no shame in doing that . . .'

Humaira stiffened at the mere suggestion.

'Everything is fine, Adeela,' she repeated, using 'that voice' that Inaya had also heard ever so often.

'I think I need to use the toilet, Badi Ma,' panted Jai, after his fourth lap around the walking track with his grandmother.

'Okay, I'll wait here for you,' said Toshi.

Jai walked slowly towards the restrooms. He didn't really need to go—he merely wanted to squander time until they could leave for lunch, instead of pointlessly circumambulating that track.

While Toshi waited for Jai to return, she gently rotated her head from side to side to release the stiffness in her neck that her arthritis sometimes caused. As she swivelled her neck to her left, she noticed a man collapse and fall to the ground, a short distance away. Toshi looked around. There was no one else in sight. She quickly walked over and helped the man to his feet. As he stood up, Toshi recognized him as the man she had met at Nabeel's Kitchen. The Pakistani. He looked at her and smiled weakly, in recognition.

'Thank you for helping me.'

'Are you all right?' she asked. 'I could get you some water from that café . . . ?' she indicated the café, which was about fifty metres away.

'Don't worry,' said Habib. 'I just got a bit dizzy—I think my blood sugar level might have dipped. It happens sometimes when I haven't eaten for a while.'

'Can I get you a sandwich?' offered Toshi.

'That's very kind of you, but I'll be fine. Honestly.'

As he said that, he staggered. Toshi reached out and steadied him.

'Please, let me accompany you to the café,' she said. 'Are you here by yourself?'

'No, my granddaughter is actually playing some practice games here.'

They walked together in an awkward silence for a bit.

'I'm sorry about troubling you like this,' said Habib. 'I've brought all my medication with me from Rawalpindi, but I often forget to take it. Humaira, my wife, always reprimands me for being so absent-minded.'

Toshi smiled. 'I can't blame her,' she said. 'So, you're from Rawalpindi? My family lived there once.'

'Ah. I assume you left during the Partition. Whereabouts did you live?'

'Near Kohati Bazar.'

'That's not very far from where we are. Perhaps you should think of visiting sometime.'

'Oh, I don't think so. There's nothing left for me to go back for,' said Toshi flatly. 'So, what brings you to London?'

'Well, I'm here for an art exhibition. It's at the Aicon Gallery this Friday,' said Habib. 'Do come if you're free.'

'You're an artist, then?'

'Some deluded people seem to think so. I live in dread of being caught out, every day,' said Habib, smiling. 'This exhibition, however, does include some truly gifted artists from the subcontinent. There will be a display of cityscapes of Rawalpindi and Amritsar. By artists from both sides of the border. Do drop by with your family, if you have an hour or so to spare.'

Toshi smiled. 'That's very kind of you to invite us.'

Just then, Jai trotted up to Toshi, 'Badi Ma, you simply have to try this quiche. It's made of the most delicious cottage cheese—you're going to love it.'

He handed her a mini quiche and took a big bite of his own.

'Hmm. Now I understand why you were away for so long, Jai,' said Toshi. 'By the way, do you remember we met this gentleman?'

Before Jai could reply, Inaya hove into his view, shoelaces undone and flyaway hair unrulier than ever.

'Daada, they're selling autographed posters of the cricketers. Can I get one, please?'

'Is your practice over, Inaya?' asked Habib.

'Yes, Daada, thanks for watching. Not!' She grinned impudently at her grandfather. It was only then that she noticed Jai and Toshi—and did a double take.

'Hey, it's *you* again!' said Inaya, crossing her arms belligerently as she turned to Jai. 'Did you send the legs of raan to your Indian bowlers yet?'

Jai cursed under his breath. Over seven billion people in the world; why was it that he always ended up running into this unsavoury sample?

Habib put an arm around Inaya's shoulders to gently rein her in, but Inaya was on a roll.

'Perhaps you could parcel over some rogan josh to up their *josh*?'

Jai spluttered with indignation, mostly at his own lack of comebacks for this annoying gadfly of a girl. Inaya watched him in wicked amusement.

'That's quite enough,' said Habib quietly to Inaya, and then turned to Toshi. 'Well, it was good meeting you, and thank you again for your help today.'

'Not at all,' said Toshi. 'Good luck with the show.'

As Habib and Inaya walked away, Jai turned to his grandmother, red-faced. 'Just who does she think she is— telling me what parcels of food to send to the Indian cricket team and stuff?'

'She's just pulling your leg, Jai. She wants to make conversation with you, and this is probably her way of breaking the ice.'

'Oh, come on, Badi Ma. I can't believe you're taking her side. Even her own granddad told her off.'

'I'm not taking her side. I'm just saying—don't let her get under your skin. I thought you handled it very well by not retaliating.'

Jai took another bite of his quiche, quite pleased that his inability to come up with a fitting response was being held up as taking the high road.

'The next time she tries that, I may not be as magnanimous,' he announced. 'Enough is enough.'

Houseful

The Puri family was now in full force in London. Rajan had also arrived for the last lap of their stay, before Arathi's assignment came to an end and they could all return to India.

Jai and Rajan were busy chopping vegetables for dinner, while Toshi cooked the lentils and rice. Arathi called to say that she was on her way home from work.

'Is our bowling really that bad, Papa?' Jai asked, as he expertly chopped the brinjal into roundels.

Rajan looked at his son in amazement, unused to this line of questioning from Jai. 'Our bowling as in . . . ?'

'I mean the Indian cricket team. Is our bowling not as good as Pakistan's?'

'Of course not. Our team is way better than Pakistan's.'

'That depends on who you ask,' interjected Toshi, smiling. 'Are the vegetables done? My dal is almost ready now and so is the rice.'

'Almost done, Ma,' said Rajan. 'I didn't know you were into cricket, Jai?'

'Oh, I'm not. There's just this annoying girl who is following me everywhere—so I need to follow cricket just so

143

I know what to say to her when she gets annoying, which is most of the time.'

'Okay, you've lost me there.'

'It's just a teenage tiff,' said Toshi with a wink, always game to add fuel to the fire.

'Pfft . . . Oh please, Badi Ma!'

'I seem to have missed quite a lot in these past few weeks,' said Rajan.

'Badi Ma has made friends with that girl's grandfather—that's why she's always taking her side.'

'Hmm. I really do seem to have missed out on quite a lot,' repeated Rajan, with a smile. 'So, you've made new friends here too, Ma?'

'There's no "too" about it, Papa,' said Jai. 'That Pesky Girl is definitely *not* my friend. And I don't think you'll like them either. They're from *Pakistan*.'

Jai said it with all the emphasis he could muster, so that his father knew full well just how treacherous a path it was that they were treading. Rajan looked rather taken aback.

'You've been meeting *Pakistanis*, Ma?'

'Well, I think they're quite all right. In fact, we've all been invited by them to an art show this Friday at the Aicon Gallery,' said Toshi. 'The girl's grandfather is an artist, and he said there will be art by leading Indian and Pakistani artists on display.'

Rajan's brows knitted together, as they tended to do when an idea didn't find favour.

'I think Arathi was planning a visit to the Sherlock Holmes museum on Baker Street on Friday, Ma,' he said. 'But we can drop you off and pick you up after, if you like?'

Toshi turned to Jai. 'You're not keen on Sherlock Holmes. Would you like to come with me, Jai?'

'There's nothing I would like less, Badi Ma,' said Jai, picturing Inaya peeping out from behind every piece of artwork, doing her jarringly hideous hyena imitation.

Acrylics and Oils

The art show was an incredibly pompous affair where the glitterati rubbed shoulders with the literati—sipping cocktails and commenting on how deeply moved they were by the ideological pathos of the acrylics and oils.

Toshi almost regretted having come. It was quite unlike her to take up an invitation like this, but the prospect of perhaps seeing Rawalpindi again, even if it was through an artist's eyes and not in person, had been the clincher.

The only problem was that since the cityscapes were mostly done in the style of abstract art, none of the paintings looked remotely like the Rawalpindi she remembered. To make matters worse, Toshi had already mistaken an art installation for a fire extinguisher and had proceeded to have an excruciatingly embarrassing conversation about it with the artist herself, so her agenda now was to simply blend into the background and wait until Rajan picked her up.

As she reached the far end of the hall, Toshi decided to park herself in front of the paintings there, given that it was comparatively less busy than the other sections of the gallery.

There was only one couple stationed there—and they nodded rapturously as Toshi approached them.

'This is such an enigmatic interpretation of life, isn't it?' said the lady, indicating a display. 'I can see the whole universe in here.'

Toshi saw nothing of the sort, nevertheless she nodded politely. The painting was another of the abstract kind. To Toshi, it merely looked like six circles, piled one on top of the other, with a line running through them. Yet, as she looked at it, she had to concede that there was something about it that seemed to draw her in. Toshi leaned in for a closer look at the painting, hoping to make some sense of it, when someone touched her lightly on her shoulder. She turned around to see Habib.

'It was very good of you to come,' he said.

The couple with Toshi seemed entirely overawed by Habib's presence.

'Oh, you're Habib Haider, aren't you? We absolutely love your art. Could we have a photograph with you please?' gushed the lady, signalling to her husband to smoothen his hair over his bald patch. 'We're *such* huge fans—in fact, we have four of your early works in our home.'

'Ah, that's more than my wife will keep in ours,' smiled Habib.

'I'm happy to click your photograph,' offered Toshi, quite tickled by this scene.

The man quickly handed his phone to Toshi and the couple happily posed with Habib, flanking him with flair. As soon as the couple had dispensed with their effusive raving and left, Toshi turned to Habib.

'Congratulations! You seem to be quite the celebrity.'

'As I said, this world is full of deluded people,' replied Habib, smiling.

'So, I take it that this is one of yours?' Toshi asked, pointing to the painting with the circles.

'Yes, and I'm told that some crazy person has offered to pay an obscene amount of money for that artwork.'

'Excellent. So, you'll be an even richer celebrity now.'

'I would be. Except that this painting is not for sale.'

'Oh. May I ask why not?'

There was a brief second of silence. 'Because it completes me,' said Habib. 'Does that make any sense?'

'Not really,' smiled Toshi. 'But I guess all you artistic lot are supposed to sound like this. Talking in circles, as they say.'

Habib threw his head back and laughed. Just then, the manager of the gallery, a young woman with a name tag and an officious look about her, rustled up to Habib.

'Excuse me, Mr Haider, could we have a few words from you please for our guests?'

'If you insist, Julia,' said Habib. 'I'll be with you in a moment.'

Julia half-smiled and bustled off. Habib looked wryly at Toshi. 'This is the bit I dread the most,' he muttered. 'I'm terrified of speaking in public. Please don't feel obliged to stay. And thanks again for coming.'

Toshi smiled. 'I'm sure you'll do a very fine job,' she said.

As Habib walked away, Toshi took one last look at the painting. She put on her spectacles and peered at the little label beside the painting.

It read:

Artist: Habib Haider
Title: TOSHI, 1961

This painting is the artist's tribute to a childhood game
he would play with his sister, Toshi. Pithoo is a game
involving seven stones. The artist chose to draw six
circles representing six stones because the seventh
stone is still in his possession—and has been ever since
he was a boy.

The ground beneath Toshi's feet seemed to shift. The room
swerved like a pendulum —and the paintings and people and
paraphernalia came crashing in on her. Gradually, the dimly
lit art gallery narrowed down to one swinging light bulb,
which cast everything in its wavering shadow. Something
inside Toshi's chest was compressing tighter and tighter. Like
hope, with its wings tied.

And that was the last thing she remembered before
she fell.

Mid-way through Habib's speech, a sudden flurry of
activity broke out at the far end of the gallery.

'Is everything all right?' asked Habib, turning to Julia.

'One of the guests fainted. She's better now. We're just
making sure she's okay. Please carry on with your talk,' she
said sotto voce, smiling reassuringly at the bewildered guests.

As soon as his speech was done, Habib hurried over to
the back of the room to collect his things, relieved that the

ordeal was over. He spotted Toshi, sitting there, looking deathly pale.

'Ah, you're still here? Is everything all right?'

Toshi looked up at him. 'Yes, yes. I'm . . . just waiting for my family to collect me,' she said.

'There's no rush to run away. Please take your time. Actually, I'm waiting for my family too—they've gone to the airport to fetch my son, you see. He's coming in from Rawalpindi today. He has finally managed to get himself some leave from work. He's a very successful banker.'

'Oh, that's nice,' said Toshi absently.

'Are you sure you're okay?'

'Yes, I am—I'm sure. I'm fine.'

Habib looked away, unconvinced. Toshi fiddled with the tassels on her shawl, then she turned to Habib.

'So, your painting . . . ' said Toshi, struggling to find the right words to phrase her question. 'How come it's called "Toshi"? Was she your sister? I mean . . . it isn't a very Muslim name, is it?'

'Oh no, she wasn't. That's just artistic license. I knew someone—he had a sister called Toshi—and my PR team thought I should give the story a spin.'

'Ah.' There was a pregnant pause before Toshi spoke again. 'And this person you knew . . . Where is he now?' Toshi was holding her breath, as if even exhaling would extinguish her feeble flicker of hope.

'He died a long time ago,' said Habib, shrugging matter-of-factly.

'I see,' said Toshi. A door slammed shut inside her and left hope out in the cold.

'Why do you ask?'

'Oh, it's nothing. It's just that I'm called Toshi too, and I had a little brother and we would play pithoo together in the gully, my brother Loki and I—and he would always hide one stone, the last one . . . '

Toshi's voice broke off.

'I bet your brother always beat you at pithoo?' said Habib, looking at her strangely. She looked up, smiling at the memory, and was about to say something, but Habib continued. 'But the only reason he won was because he had three thumbs, right?'

He held up his left hand. Toshi just stared at it, speechless.

'Tar . . . Tarlok . . . ? Loki?' she whispered, almost fearful to even give voice to the hope welling inside her.

Habib nodded, tears streaming down his face. He reached into his pocket and took out an oval, olive-coloured pebble that resembled a bulbul's egg.

'I've carried this with me every day of my life,' he said. 'I call it my rock of hope. Do you recognize this pebble from our game of pithoo, Toshi di?'

Toshi sat still as if she were frozen in time, hearing her name being spoken again by her brother, whom she believed to have been dead all these years. She felt something warm and bright rekindle deep within her, though its flames were tentative and tenuous.

'But . . . but your name is Habib . . . '

Habib nodded.

'Today, I am Habib Haider. It's a long story . . . '

Toshi felt a dam breaking deep within her. Her grief, held back for a lifetime, finally found its release.

'I'm listening, Loki,' she said through her tears.

Habib came over and sat down beside her.

'I owe my life to some *farishtas,* two guardian angels, who came into my world—after I lost all of you. One of them was called Rahmat Bibi and the other, Rukhsana . . . '

Rukhsana

It was Sunday, the day that Rukhsana Haider would visit the orphanage near their home. Three young children crowded around Rukhsana's knee, almost on her lap, listening wide-eyed as she told them the story of Sabu, the naughty cat. Mrs Rao, the manager of the orphanage came over, smiling at the sight of their rapt little faces.

'I hate to tear them away from their favourite person, but it's dinner time,' she said. 'Come on, children, give Rukhsana Aapa a hug and go wash your hands.'

The children hugged Rukhsana and skipped off to eat.

'Thank you so much for bringing in these sweets and presents for the children. You don't know just how much it means to them,' said Mrs Rao.

Rukhsana smiled. 'It means far more to me, Jayaji. Children are such a joy.'

Quite subconsciously, she tenderly patted her expectant belly.

'When is the baby due, Rukhsana?'

'Just one month to go, Jayaji,' she smiled. 'I had better head home now. Javed and Ammi will be waiting for me. I'll see you next Sunday.'

Rukhsana emerged from the orphanage building and had barely taken ten steps when she was caught up in a turbulent wave of angry rioters, charging down the street, armed with axes, swords and staffs.

'Har har Mahadev! Har har Mahadev!' they roared. As they rushed past her, one of them roughly shoved her aside.

'Ya Allah!' cried Rukhsana, instinctively, as she tried to regain her balance.

A member of the mob overheard her and walked towards her menacingly. 'She's one of them!' he roared, his bloodshot eyes spewing hatred.

He grabbed her arm and viciously pushed her, face down, into the gutter by the side of the road. As she fell, she felt something wet and warm seeping out. A dull ache throbbed in her heart. A yearning for something that should have been hers to hold and love but which she now knew was not to be. All she felt was an emptiness. A clawing, hollow emptiness. And then, everything went dark.

Javed jumped out of the taxi and knocked on the orphanage door. He couldn't wait to get Rukhsana and Ammi to safety, away from this chaos. Ghanshyam had said that a mob was headed to Azad Nagar. Things were getting worse with each passing hour. They needed to leave New Delhi as soon as possible.

'Is Rukhsana here, Jayaji?' he asked, as Mrs Rao opened the door.

'No. She left a while ago. Is everything all right, Javed?'

Javed left without another word. He walked in a daze, desperately trying to keep his worst thoughts at bay. Javed was spotted at this moment by Raghu, Ghanshyam's son, on his way home after his shift at the nearby government hospital. Jumping off his bicycle, Raghu rushed over to Javed's side.

It was half an hour before they found Rukhsana, still lying in the ditch, barely conscious. Javed stood rooted to the spot, unable to come to grips with what he was seeing. Raghu immediately bent down to help Rukhsana. He felt her pulse—it was still present, although very faint.

'Dr Khurana is on duty at the hospital,' said Raghu. 'I used to be his compounder. I'm sure he'll see Rukhsana Bibi on priority.'

Javed nodded, his mind still unable to wrap itself around what had happened. He just sat there holding his wife's hand.

Twenty minutes later, they were outside Dr Khurana's consulting room. Upon seeing Javed and Raghu carrying Rukhsana, Dr Khurana's eyes widened in alarm. He quickly ushered them in, glancing nervously around to ensure that no one had seen the Muslim couple. In these dark times, even giving medical attention to Muslims could cost him his job—or life, even.

Dr Khurana carried out a quick examination of Rukhsana and motioned to his staff to prepare for surgery.

'We need to operate immediately,' he told Javed. 'The baby is almost at full term.'

'Yes, our child is due next month,' said Javed, almost to himself. The clock in the nearby church's steeple struck six.

'I'll go and bring Arjumand Bibiji here,' said Raghu. 'The hospital is probably the safest place for all of you to spend the night, Javed Sahib.'

Javed nodded absently, anxious eyes on the doors of the operation theatre, just waiting for Dr Khurana to emerge. After what seemed like an eternity to Javed, Dr Khurana walked out. Javed stood up as he saw him.

'Her vitals are stable now; she's going to be all right,' said the doctor. 'But I'm sorry. Although we tried our best, we couldn't save the baby.'

Javed stared at the floor, his senses felt scrambled. He could almost taste the metallic bittersweet emotion coursing through his veins. Rukhsana was alive. That was the only thing that mattered. But this was the second child she had lost. The grief would devastate her. He shut his eyes, as if to shut out the thought.

'Thank you for saving Rukhsa—' he started to say, when Dr Khurana cut him off.

'She is lucky to have survived that, but neither of you is safe outside. It isn't advisable for you to return home tonight. I suggest that you both stay the night in the hospital.'

Javed looked defeated, like nothing mattered any more. 'May I see Rukhsana now, doctor?'

'She's sleeping off the effects of anaesthesia. Give it a little while, son.'

When Arjumand walked into the hospital, she took one look at Rukhsana and Javed and realized she had lost her unborn grandchild. The child for whom she had made a pilgrimage to Ajmer Sharif.

Rukhsana broke down in tears upon seeing her and collapsed in her mother-in-law's arms. Arjumand squeezed her eyes shut as she held Rukhsana. She could feel the dampness of Rukhsana's tears on her shoulder; the body that had been counting down to joy, now heaving, heartbroken. She fought back her own tears, willing herself to be strong for the grief-stricken girl in her arms.

'If it is God's will, you will have many more children, my Rukhsana,' she said. Arjumand's eyes met Javed's. The emptiness in his eyes chilled her to the marrow. She enveloped Javed in her embrace, holding both her son and her daughter-in-law. And in that moment of grief, the decision that she never thought she would make, was made.

Arjumand Haider would leave her home, her India.

Rahmat Bibi

17 August 1947
Rawalpindi, Pakistan

While Tarlok waited for Toshi to return with her doll to referee their game of pithoo, he picked up the green pebble from the ground, expertly tossing it in the air and catching it. In the distance, he could hear the chants, 'Allahu Akbar!' The sound seemed to be drawing closer.

From the other end of the road, Tarlok could see his father returning home. Relieved, he started to call out to him, but before he could say a word, someone swooped him up and started running. Tarlok tried to scream, but a large hand covered his mouth and most of his face.

'Shhh . . . Be quiet!' the man hissed.

With his one partly uncovered eye, Tarlok could just about make out that the man who was bearing him away was wearing the lace skullcap worn by Muslims.

The man looked around furtively and dived into a small alleyway. He went through a maze of narrow alleys before finally slowing down. The man peered through the window of one of the houses where an elderly woman knelt on a prayer mat, offering namaz. Pushing the door open, he gently lowered Tarlok to the floor. Tarlok was all set to scream for help but then, much to his shock, realized that he recognized the man. It was Abrar Chachu, his father's childhood friend. Abrar bent down to Tarlok.

'Go inside, beta,' he said. 'Rahmat Aapa will take care of you. And I'll bring the rest of your family here as well. You just wait with her quietly, all right? And here, keep this with you.'

He drew off his skullcap and handed it to Tarlok who hesitantly took it. Abrar gave him a quick hug and left.

Five minutes later, Rahmat Bibi finished her namaz and looked up to find a frightened little boy standing by the door. Tarlok flinched as she hobbled towards him.

'You're Baldev's little boy, aren't you, beta?' she asked, gently. 'How did you get here? Is Baldev outside?'

Before Tarlok could respond, there came a loud banging on the door. Rahmat Bibi went over to the window, drew back the curtain and peeped out. It was a crowd of angry insurgents. She looked around in panic and noticed Abrar's skullcap in Tarlok's hand.

'Put the cap on, beta, and sit there on the prayer mat,' she said.

She opened the door, adjusting her headscarf as she did so. The mob almost knocked her frail body down as they charged inside, looking around like rabid animals. One of them burst into her kitchen while another went towards her bedroom. They searched the whole house—behind the curtains, under the beds.

'What are you looking for?' asked Rahmat Bibi.

'There are kaafirs among us. Some of our own people are hiding these godforsaken Hindus and Sikhs. We have to find them and finish them off.'

The leader of the mob looked around the house. He saw Tarlok seated on the prayer mat, Abrar's skullcap on his little head.

'Apologies, Aapa. It looks like we disturbed your namaz. I hope Allah will forgive us,' he said.

Rahmat Bibi shook her head sadly. 'I hope so too for what you are doing is certainly not Allah's bidding.'

The man glared at her.

'We'll be back,' he said. 'Let us know if you see anything or anyone suspicious.'

The rioters left as suddenly as they had erupted into the house, leaving behind a hiatus of shell-shocked silence.

Rahmat Bibi went over to Tarlok. He was trembling with fear, having seen the threatening men with their sharp knives and weapons.

'It will be all right,' Rahmat Bibi said gently. She secured the windows and doors as quickly as she could and took him into the kitchen. She tried to pick him up with her old, feeble arms to seat him on the kitchen counter, but the effort made her wheeze and she doubled up, coughing.

Tarlok quietly went and got her a cup of water. She took it gratefully from him and drank it. Rahmat Bibi warmed a cup of milk for Tarlok, took out a tin of rusks and offered them to him. He looked hesitant but then took both—dipping the rusk in the milk, just as he did at home.

'When will my Biji and Papaji come to get me?' he asked Rahmat Bibi.

'They should be here any time now, beta,' she lied.

Abrar Ansari headed for his friend, Baldev Sahni's house, to assure them that Tarlok was safe and to try and get the rest of the family to safety too. The sun was setting and Abrar slipped into the shadows, hoping to make it into the side entrance of the Sahni house, so as to avoid the large mob on the main street.

He had almost reached the door, when one of the insurgents also entered the lane and spotted Abrar. Seeing Abrar stealthily step into a home with a prominent tulsi plant in its courtyard, he mistook Abrar to be a Hindu. 'Look, a kaafir!' he cried, beckoning to the rest of the mob.

'I'm not Hindu; I'm Muslim, believe me!' Abrar pleaded. But the rioters were in no mood to listen. The man who had spotted Abrar brought his axe sharply down on Abrar's skull. The crack resonated through the air. Abrar collapsed in a bloody heap. One rioter doused him in kerosene while another set him alight.

'Allahu Akbar!' their triumphant cries rang out while Abrar Ansari burned.

It was several months before Rahmat Bibi came to know about the death of her brother. She kept expecting Abrar to drop in on her unannounced as he so often did, bringing gulab jamuns or jalebis, but as time passed, she gave up hope that his familiar footsteps would ever approach her door. She continued to wake up every morning with the first call of the muezzin, but, had it not been for the little boy whom Allah had left in her care, she might not have had the will to get out of bed. Three months had passed, and there was no news about Tarlok's parents either. Rahmat Bibi had made very discreet inquiries about the whereabouts of the Sahnis, but nobody seemed to know where they were. Rahmat Bibi was seriously worried. How much longer would she be able to conceal this little boy in her home? She was getting on in years herself. As she sat for her evening namaz, her only *dua* to Allah was: Please look after this boy and keep him safe.

As if in answer to those prayers, Rahmat Bibi had a visit from her closest friend, Suraiya, who informed her of a certain Haider family who had migrated into Rawalpindi from New Delhi, during the wrench of the Partition.

'Poor Rukhsana Haider,' said Suraiya. 'Apparently, she lost her baby in the riots,' Then lowering her voice, she continued, 'I've heard that she can never conceive a child now.'

Rahmat Bibi looked at the lonely little boy sitting by the window and looking out at the street.

'God works in mysterious ways,' she said. 'There is sometimes a bigger plan that we are not aware of. Perhaps she may yet have a child—who knows?'

Later that evening, Rahmat Bibi took Tarlok on her knee. 'Beta, you don't need to hide here anymore. Allah has sent new parents for you. And from today, your name will be Habib. Do you know what that means?'

Tarlok shook his head. 'It means "beloved". You are going to be their very beloved son,' said Rahmat Bibi, kissing his forehead. 'But before that, there's something I need to do to you. It will hurt a little, but this pain will be worth it.'

After spending a few months in the refugee camps near Rawalpindi, the Haiders were allocated a house that had been abandoned by a Hindu family. It was a very basic home, nowhere near as grand as Musaafir Khaana, the home they had left behind, but they were grateful for a roof over their heads.

Rahmat Bibi was filled with trepidation as she approached the Haiders' new home. What if she was found out? What if the Haiders discovered that this child was not born to Muslim parents? She had arranged for his circumcision to be carried out by her nephew who was a doctor, swearing him to secrecy, but what if the truth was somehow exposed?

She knocked timidly on the door, but as she waited, she lost her nerve and turned to leave. Just then, Javed Haider opened the door.

'Yes, can I help you?' he said, rather surprised to see old Rahmat Bibi on the doorstep, holding a little child by the hand.

'Is Rukhsana Bibi home? I'm Rahmat Azam, an old friend of her family.'

Javed looked perplexed, never having heard the name earlier, but he invited her in all the same.

'Do have a seat. I'll let Rukhsana know you're here.'

As she waited for Rukhsana, Rahmat Bibi's fears resurfaced. But when Rukhsana entered the drawing room, one look at her gentle face set Rahmat Bibi's apprehensions at rest. She knew she was doing the right thing. There was a kindness in Rukhsana's eyes—the tenderness with which she looked at Tarlok filled Rahmat Bibi with hope.

'I'm sorry to barge in like this, uninvited . . . ' she began.

'Not at all,' said Rukhsana. 'In fact, all of you are the ones who have taken us in, uninvited, into a new city, a new country . . . ' She broke off as her voice faltered.

Rahmat Bibi took Tarlok by the hand and drew him into her lap.

'Rukhsana Bibi, I hear that you have a loving heart—and this child here, Habib, needs compassion more than anybody else. He lost his parents in the riots—had I been younger, I would have gladly reared him as my own . . . '

Rukhsana knelt by the sofa, with arms outstretched, 'Come to me, Habib. Come, my child.'

Tarlok clutched Rahmat Bibi's shalwar and sat glued to her lap.

'Come to me, Habib,' Rukhsana repeated.

'My name is not Habib, it's Tarlok,' said the little boy.

Rahmat Bibi's face went pale. Flustered, she rose and made to leave the room. 'I'm so sorry. I didn't mean to mislead you . . . We'll take our leave.'

'One moment,' Rukhsana's voice stayed them when Rahmat Bibi was almost at the door, Tarlok's little hand in hers. 'You've visited our home for the first time—please don't leave empty-handed.'

Rukhsana picked up a handful of nuts from a salver on the teapoy and approached Tarlok. She knelt and offered these to him.

'Do you like pistachios and almonds?' she asked. 'They make you big and strong, you know.'

A teardrop rolled down Tarlok's small face. Through his blurry eyes, he could almost see his Biji sitting, hand extended, telling him to have his pistachios and almonds if he wanted to grow up and be big and strong. He could hear her call after him, as he ran off to catch the school bus with Toshi, thrusting the nuts into his hand as he clambered on.

He blinked his tears away and saw that this lady was not his Biji. Rukhsana held out her arms to him.

'I know I'm not your mother, but I would be the happiest person alive if you were to be my son.'

Rahmat Bibi's eyes filled with grateful tears. She gently unclenched Tarlok's fist from the folds of her shalwar and gave his hand into Rukhsana's.

Rukhsana kissed his plump little hand and hugged the little boy. It was as if destiny had been defied and she had been given what she had been denied.

'Habib Haider, my son, I will love you with every breath I take,' she whispered.

Threads

'And that's how I grew up as Habib Haider.'

Toshi was too overcome to say anything. It seemed to her like a latticework of fragmented memories had found a thread that bound them together, and she held on to it tightly, too scared to let go.

'Loki, did you ever see Biji and Papaji again . . . ?'

Habib shook his head.

'I was told that all of you had died . . . ' he began, his voice thick with feeling, the words stuck to the back of his throat.

'But didn't Zulaikha Baaji tell you that Bade Papa, Badi Ma and I had gone to India?' asked Toshi. 'It was she and Khalid Chacha who helped us get on that train. Did you not meet them again?'

Habib shook his head again.

'All I heard was that they had disappeared. Some people thought that they had also been killed. For helping kaafirs,' he said quietly.

Toshi's eyes brimmed with tears.

'I still cannot believe that life has brought us together again, Loki. It has been over sixty years. We have so much lost time to catch up on. I can't explain the thrill of saying your name—and knowing that you're there. There hasn't been a day that I haven't regretted that day when I left you out in that gully all by yourself, Loki,' she said, her voice breaking.

Habib looked at his sister and saw beneath her greying hair, the same ten-year-old girl neatly piling the pebbles.

'I know,' he said softly.

They sat there, talking about the paths their lives had taken them on, trying to fill in the gaps of six decades.

'Where do I begin? There's so much I want to ask,' said Toshi.

Habib smiled, 'My turn first. So, Jai is your grandson. Who did you marry, Toshi di? How many children do you have?'

Toshi sighed, 'I wish you had met my husband. His name was Prakash Puri. He was kind and good-hearted, just like you, Loki. And I have a son, Jai's father—his name is Rajan.'

'Is he here, in London? Is this where you live? When can I meet him?'

Just then, Rajan walked up to them. 'Sorry, Ma,' he apologized, his quizzical smile flashing over the old gentleman seated by his mother. 'There was a really long queue to get into the museum. I hope we haven't kept you waiting too long.'

'Not at all, Rajan. The wait was well worth it,' replied Toshi, smiling.

Too Familiar

'So, what is this big lunch about, Ma?' asked Rajan. They were seated in a Chinese restaurant, decorated in bold reds, with a swan motif on practically every imaginable surface.

'It's just a small celebration as a family—and besides, it was Arathi's birthday, so we need to mark the occasion,' said Toshi. She looked happier than Rajan had seen her look in a very long time.

'Shall we order?' asked Jai. He found all these discussions rather pointless. Big lunches were meant for eating. Period.

'Yes, why not?' said Arathi, smiling indulgently. 'Try and catch a waiter's attention please, Jai.'

As Jai turned around to try and catch the waiter's eye, his attention was drawn to someone else instead. He groaned. This could *not* be happening. Pesky Girl and her family were in the same restaurant—and as if that weren't bad enough, they seemed to be heading towards their table.

'Hello,' said Habib, 'We meet again.'

Toshi smiled at him. 'What a coincidence,' she said—which it certainly wasn't, as Habib and she had decided to 'bump' into each other at this restaurant with their families, so that they could break their news to them. In stages.

Arathi stiffened at seeing the Pakistani family again.

'We're all in attendance now—the whole *khaandaan*,' said Habib, with a smile. 'I'd like you to meet my son, Irfan. And this is my wife Humaira and her sister Adeela.'

'It's wonderful to meet you all,' said Toshi. 'And this is my son, Rajan—you met him briefly at the art gallery—the rest of us probably look familiar.'

'Too familiar,' muttered Jai, under his breath.

'Are you talking to yourself?' asked Inaya.

'Er, no,' said Jai. 'You must be imagining things.' Okay, not the greatest comeback, thought Jai, but it was a start.

'Lovely,' said Habib. 'So, we'll let you get on with your lunch. But perhaps we could all have dessert together later. We might as well plan it out this time since we seem to be bumping into each other everywhere?'

He looked around at the group's stunned faces, quietly amused. No one seemed to be displaying any enthusiasm whatsoever.

'We're leaving for Pakistan in a few days, so it's unlikely that we'll see each other again,' he continued, 'And Inaya and I have discovered this fabulous little gelato place, which is less than five minutes away . . . '

Jai perked up visibly at the mention of gelato. 'Gelato sounds good,' he said, and regretted his words as soon as they were out of his mouth.

Arathi gave him a withering look.

'Perfect, it's decided then,' said Habib. 'Enjoy your lunch.'

Humaira was positively seething as they walked to their table.

'What were you thinking, Habib?' she asked through gritted teeth.

'Yes, Abba, what were you thinking?' echoed Irfan.

'That was pretty random, Daada,' said Inaya.

'I think it was a lovely gesture, Bhaijaan,' trilled Adeela.

Humaira clucked her tongue, making her displeasure known, loud and clear. 'Well, you can go ahead then, I won't be joining this merry get-together,' she said.

Adeela shook her head sadly. 'It's all right, Bhaijaan— Inaya and you carry on. Humaira Aapa won't let me hear the end of it if I go with you. We'll see you at home after you've had your gelatos.'

Things weren't too different at the Puris table either, where Arathi and Rajan turned on Jai.

'Really, Jai?' said Arathi. 'After all that moaning about "Pesky Girl", you subject us all to sharing ice cream with them?'

Rajan looked to his mother. 'If it's okay by you, Ma—can you take Jai and join them for this gelato thing? Arathi and I had planned on doing some shopping for gifts after lunch.'

'All right, it's just us then, Jai,' said Toshi. 'Brace yourself.' She smiled to herself.

Little did Jai know what he was in for.

Fireflies

As soon as the four of them had got a table at the gelato café, Toshi took a deep breath and looked at her brother as a signal to say she was going to launch into the story. With the slightest nod of his head, Habib told her to go ahead.

Toshi turned to Jai, who was examining the menu card with the single-minded focus that Roger Federer displayed before serving an ace.

'Jai, do you remember the story I told you about Tarlok?' asked his grandmother, gently touching his arm. Jai looked up at her. He remembered it vividly. After his encounter with Ansh and the gang, he had often thought about Badi Ma's brave little brother, who lost his life in the Partition.

'Yes, Badi Ma, I do remember.'

'Well—this is Tarlok, my younger brother.'

Jai looked at Habib and then at his grandmother.

'Good one, Badi Ma!' he said with a laugh.

'I'm not joking, Jai,' said Toshi. Something about her voice made Jai sit up straighter.

'So, you're saying that Pesk—Inaya's grandfather is your brother?'

Both Toshi and Habib nodded.

Both Inaya and Jai were struck speechless. Jai was the first of the two to recover.

'But you said your brother was . . . dead, Badi Ma.'

'Hold on—did you just say that you two are sister and brother?' Inaya butted in, her reaction slightly delayed.

Habib and Toshi looked at each other and nodded again, amused by their grandchildren's startled expressions.

'That's right, Jai. I was mistaken all my life. Tarlok is alive and well,' said Toshi.

'Who's this Tarlok? My grandfather's name is Habib,' said Inaya.

'It's a long story, Inaya,' said Habib.

'Badi Ma, you do know that he is Muslim right?' whispered Jai conspiratorially, although he was loud enough for everyone to hear. He could just about picture his parents having a hissy fit when they would learn about this new development.

'Yes. He is Muslim,' said Toshi. 'And I have grown up as a Hindu. But the bond we share is far stronger than the faith we practise.'

A lightbulb seemed to come on in Jai's head. He let out a long, satisfied sigh, 'Ah, now I get it. This is some kind of candid camera joke that you both have planned, right?'

'No, it isn't, Jai,' said Toshi.

'In fact, if anything, life has played the biggest joke on us, all these years,' added Habib.

Jai looked entirely flummoxed. So, Badi Ma now apparently had a Muslim brother who was alive and tucked away in Pakistan, who then turned out be the grandfather of Pesky Girl.

Meanwhile, Inaya was processing her thoughts, in the context of what this meant to her. 'Hold on a second—how come you never mentioned that you had a sister, Daada?' she asked. 'Or am I the only one who doesn't know about this?'

'You're the only one who knows, Inaya,' said Habib.

'But how come your sister is from India, Daada?' she said. 'Do you think we're related to Jhulan Goswami too?' she added, as an appealing afterthought dawned on her.

If her grandfather was going to suddenly spring long-lost relatives from across the border at her, he might have chosen better, she thought to herself. This Jai was a complete waste of space, in Inaya's opinion. All he did was think about food and eat it. No interest whatsoever in cricket—or any sport for that matter.

'No, Inaya, I don't think we're related to Jhulan,' said Habib, smiling. 'Inaya's a champion cricketer, by the way,' he added, turning to his sister.

'Ah, that's wonderful,' said Toshi, reaching forward to give a startled Inaya a hug.

Jai glowered at his grandmother. Why was she being so affectionate towards Pesky Girl?

'Jai is a budding chef—and he draws really well too—just like you, Tarlok,' said Toshi proudly.

Jai cringed. Why was Badi Ma now suddenly comparing him to Inaya's grandfather? It was just weird. But then he remembered that Inaya's grandfather was his grandmother's brother. Apparently.

'So, do you live in Rawalpindi?' asked Jai.

'Yes,' said Habib. 'Not very far from the house that your Badi Ma and I grew up in.'

'You didn't answer my question, Daada. How come your sister is from India?' repeated Inaya.

'Well your great-grandparents adopted me, Inaya—and we were all given to believe that my birth family—my grandparents, parents and sister—had been killed in the riots that followed the Partition.'

'Hmm. So Daadi knows nothing about your sister?' continued Inaya.

'No, she doesn't,' said Habib, smiling. 'This is going to be interesting.'

'Get ready for World War III,' said Inaya.

'Oh, don't worry. We're in the same boat. Wait until my parents find out that Badi Ma has a Muslim brother, that too from Pakistan; all hell will break loose,' said Jai with morbid glee.

Toshi gave Jai a playful whack on his arm. 'So, she still does that arm whacking, huh?' said Habib, watching them with a smile. 'And Jai, is she still as competitive when you play games?'

'Oh, you have no idea . . . ' started Jai, and then his voice trailed off. He was still trying to grapple with the fact that this actually *was* his grandmother's brother, someone who knew her idiosyncrasies—probably even better than he did. He felt a pang of possessiveness, almost. No one was allowed to know Badi Ma better than he did.

Habib turned to Toshi. 'We didn't get to finish our conversation that day, Toshi di. Do you all live in London?'

'No, we live in New Delhi, and you must plan a visit soon, Loki.'

'Life is so strange, Toshi di,' said Habib. 'My adopted parents migrated from New Delhi to Rawalpindi, and you did the reverse.'

'All the more reason for you to come,' said Toshi. 'Tell me, is that pomegranate tree still there . . . the one we used to steal from? And do the fireflies still dance over the canal at night? And who lives in our house now?'

'Yes, that tree and the fireflies are still very much there. Sadly, however, our house never got rebuilt after it burned down. They've built some small shops in its place. But what our neighbourhood is known for now is the first ever café outlet of Nabeel's Kitchen. In fact, Nabeel Said is the reason we're in London right now. She is sponsoring Inaya's tape-ball tournament.'

Jai looked up sharply.

'Nabeel Said of Nabeel's Kitchen fame is spon—THAT Nabeel Said?' A new-found respect for Inaya crept into Jai's voice.

'*You* know of Nabeel Said?' returned Inaya, equally astounded. For the first time in her life, she looked at Jai with something approaching awe.

'She has been my hero ever since I read about her in a magazine four years ago,' said Jai. 'I want to open a chain of cafés like her one day, and serve up food that reminds us of our grandmothers' cooking, but with a modern twist—just like she does. Why do you think I was so desperate to try her haleem rolls?'

'I just assumed that you were a glutton,' shrugged Inaya.

Jai ignored her and carried on, 'I would kill to get the recipe for them.'

'Would you like to meet her?'

Jai's eyes widened as his head swam in a heady cocktail of disbelief and anticipation, 'Can you actually introduce me to Nabeel Said?'

'Sure. What are you doing tomorrow afternoon? Drop in during my match. She'll be there,' said Inaya, coolly.

Meanwhile, Toshi and Habib hadn't heard a word of the conversation between their grandchildren, engrossed as they were in catching up on the three score years that they had lost out on. Jai looked at them and then turned back to Inaya. 'Do you know this makes us cousins?' he whispered.

'What does?' asked Inaya.

'Our grandparents being siblings makes us cousins,' Jai repeated.

'That's really weird. But you know what—I feel a bit sorry for them. I mean, I don't have a brother—Zain's probably the closest I have to a brother. And he's pretty annoying, but I just can't imagine not seeing him for the rest of my life.'

'Is Zain your cousin?'

'He's actually my neighbour. He's quite a pain on most days. But he's the one who secretly lent me his cricket bat when Abba wouldn't buy me one, and he'd let me watch him at the nets when he was being coached. That's how I learnt most of my cricket. So, he's all right, I guess.'

'He doesn't sound too bad. So, you like Jhulan Goswami, huh?'

'Do you know her?' gushed Inaya.

'I know *of* her, even though I'm not a cricket fan. If you come to India, I'll travel with you to go and meet her, if you like?'

'You'd do that?'

'Sure. I've always wanted to try authentic Bengali food.'

Inaya rolled her eyes heavenwards in a mute prayer for strength.

'I actually have so many Indian cricketers whom I want to meet,' she said. 'Wouldn't it be so much fun if I could actually come?'

'Do it. My parents could help arrange your visa. And now we're family. You have even more reason to visit.'

'You should also come to Pakistan,' said Inaya. 'Come and see Nabeel's Kitchen, if nothing else!'

'That sounds great! And it needn't end with that. You know what we should do?' said Jai, an idea taking shape in his head.

'Don't tell me you're planning to secretly live in her kitchen forever . . . '

'Do you think I'm crazy?'

'Well, you do have some bizarre ideas.'

'Jai and Inaya,' interrupted Toshi. 'We need your help. We need to break the news to the rest of the family. Any suggestions as to the best way we can do this?'

'Do it on the day we're leaving,' said Jai. 'Let's enjoy the rest of the holiday.'

Inaya burst out laughing. 'I agree with him,' she said. 'For once.'

'Be nice, Inaya,' chided her grandfather.

'That's like asking a fish to climb a tree,' said Jai.

'I'm sure that even fish know more about cricket than you do,' retorted Inaya.

'Breaking news: Cricket does not make the world go round. There are many other interests that people have,' retaliated Jai.

'What do you have against each other?' said Habib, shaking his head in despair.

'It's a long story, Daada,' replied Inaya, grinning.

'So, can we meet tomorrow as well?' asked Toshi.

'Of course,' said Habib.

'Do we have to?' groaned Jai and Inaya, almost in perfect synchrony.

Four's Company

The next morning, the foursome met again on the pretext of a shopping expedition. While Toshi and Habib chatted over a cup of tea in the basement café at Marks & Spencer, Jai and Inaya strolled aimlessly through the aisles to pass the time. There was pet food on one side and detergents on the other. Inaya distractedly picked up a can of cat food and looked at the ingredients.

'Whitefish. Botanically boosted by nettle, cranberries, fennel and chamomile. Yuck! Do cats even like this stuff?'

Jai barely heard her, consumed as he was with an idea that had refused to leave his head.

'Listen Inaya, I've been thinking . . .'

Inaya grimaced at these words. She really didn't need Jai's thoughts at this time. She had enough of her own to grapple with. Besides, she needed to be at practice rather than be Daada's chaperone while he met his long-lost sister to plot about how they were going to break the news to the rest of the family.

Jai, oblivious to all of Inaya's woes, was still talking. 'I've been thinking that we should start Peace-ing It Together,' he said.

'Start piecing what together?'

'You know—start a club that does the opposite of what the Partition did.'

Inaya looked at him, all at sea. 'What are you on about, Jai?'

'Peace-ing spelt with P-E-A-C-E, not P-I-E-C-E. We could start a movement, build a bridge, you know, to bring us together again,' said Jai. He was getting really excited now with his seedling notion and began pacing rapidly between the cans of cat and dog food. It was when he reached the section with hamster food that he got truly inspired.

'This is what we'd do. We'd get people from both sides of the border who have relatives and friends and homes and memories on the other side to get to meet each other again and revisit what they left behind. Imagine how happy it would make them.'

'Okay, but first, can you stop moving like a ball in a tennis match? Watching you is giving me a headache,' said Inaya. 'And secondly, how would we manage to do this without getting arrested? Are you planning on smuggling people across, wrapped in carpets? Because I don't know if you've noticed, but our countries' governments haven't been the best of friends for a very long time.'

'Yes, but that's the governments, right? Let them carry on with their own agendas—and let's get on with ours.'

'Yeah, like that's so simple, right?'

Jai stared hard at the fish food section, and it dawned on him that it wasn't all that hard.

'Things are easier now with the internet. This is going to be an online movement, Inaya,' he said. 'We're going to begin with Facebook and it's going to gradually spread and grow—just you wait and see.'

'Whatever,' said Inaya. To her, this sounded like a hare-brained scheme, but she decided to humour Jai, since he had promised to help her meet Jhulan Goswami.

'I'm going to start tomorrow. Maybe we can ask Nabeel Said to help us?' said Jai, looking hopefully at Inaya.

'Did you know that cats like nettle?' asked Inaya, pretending that she hadn't heard him. 'Or that hamster food has locust beans added in it for flavour?'

'Locust beans?' said Jai, thrown off the track. 'What on earth are they?'

'Result,' thought Inaya. Boys were so easy to manipulate.

Howzat?

Despite Inaya's lukewarm reception to his idea, Jai desperately wanted to start this online movement. The only problem was that he hadn't been able to figure out how to kick-start it. He sat staring at the computer with absolutely no clue where to begin. For want of something better to do, Jai started browsing through the photographs he had taken with the Nikon camera that Rustom had given him. Most were of food, predictably. But there were a few photographs of people, if they happened to be around the food.

He came across one of Badi Ma and her brother at the gelato café. They looked so happy. He had rarely seen his grandmother look this happy in all her life. He copied it on to a poster format and printed it out. He looked at it, wondering what to write. He wrote a few words, struck them out and wrote a few more, only to strike them out as well. Finally, he just gave up and went to bed.

A little later, Toshi came into the kitchen to ensure that she had turned off the gas. It was something she did every night before going to bed. Then, invariably, she'd wake up with a start in the middle of the night and check again, just in case. Having reassured herself that all was well, Toshi was on her way back to bed when she found the half-made poster lying on the kitchen table. She looked at the many words that Jai had scratched out. She picked up the pen and wrote: 'I am an Indian. And my sibling is Pakistani. Can you tell who is from which country?'

She stood up, checked the gas once more and switched off the lights in the kitchen.

In his room, Jai was tossing and turning in bed. He squinted in the dark to look at the time. It was 3 a.m. Jai sat up. His throat felt parched—he headed to the kitchen and got himself a glass of water. He was drinking it when he spotted Badi Ma's handwritten words on the poster. He read it to himself and then out loud. This was perfect. This was exactly the sort of thing he needed to take his plan forward.

Just then, his laptop pinged. It was a message from Rustom.

'Hey Jai. Why aren't you ever online? And when are you coming back? It's super dull here.'

Jai's eyes lit up. If there was one person who could help him with this, it was Rustom. He had won competitions for catchy captions, after all. Never mind whether they were his own or not. He sat down at his computer and messaged Rustom.

'Hey Rusty. What's up?'

'Wow. That was quick! You've never ever responded to any message that fast. And why are you even awake at this hour?'

'I need your help, Rusty. You're good with captions, right? You won that contest and stuff. I urgently need captions for some photographs.'

'Ah. I knew there'd be some catch to this rapid response time.'

'Listen, this is really important, Rusty. My grandmother has found her long-lost brother—and he's Pakistani.'

'Nice one. My grandmother has also found her long-lost Pakistani brother—and he's Imran Khan. Howzat?'

'I'm serious, Rusty.'

'Have you hit your head on something hard, Jai? I know it's not waking hours for you, but you're not making any sense.'

'I know it all sounds crazy, but it's true, Rusty. And now I have to figure out a way to get many more people like my grandma and her brother to reconnect with their family and friends whom they had to leave behind in the Partition.'

Jai stared at the computer screen waiting for Rustom's reply, while Rustom let this sink in.

'Okay. This is huge. And slightly crazy. But send me the photographs. I'll see what I can do.'

'Thanks, Rusty!'

Jai grinned happily.

A little while later, Rustom had sent Jai some options for captions over an email. Jai read them aloud to himself.

'Option 1: They drew a line, but they couldn't divide us.

Option 2: Some bonds defy all borders . . . '

He had barely finished reading the first two options, when Rustom messaged.

'So, what did you think of them, Jai?'

'Did you think of these yourself, Rusty? Or are they "borrowed" as usual?'

'You just concern yourself with using the captions that you like. You ask way too many unnecessary questions, instead of thanking me for taking the time to support all your daft schemes.'

Jai grinned and placed Rustom's captions alongside the poster that Badi Ma had written on and took a photograph. Then he created a Facebook page called 'Peace-ing It Together', uploaded the photograph and went back to bed.

The Little Green Dot

A few days later, Jai woke up to at least three dozen messages from Rustom, who was waiting for Jai to show up online.

'What's wrong with you, Jai? I've been waiting for ages!' messaged Rusty, the minute he saw a little green dot appear next to Jai's name.

'Rusty, you do you realize there's a four-and-a-half-hour time difference, don't you?' Jai typed back, rubbing his eyes.

'Well, wake up, sleeping beauty, and check out the storm.'

Jai looked out of the window. It seemed like a perfectly calm day—there was barely even a breeze.

'Where's the storm? In New Delhi?'

'On your Facebook page, Jai! Indians and Pakistanis and Bangladeshis from all over the world have been posting on your new Facebook page.'

'About what?'

'About that poster you posted. Of your Badi Ma and her brother. Now they're all

posting photos of people and possessions they
left behind in the Partition. Some people
have started a "Guess Where I'm From?" quiz
and . . . '

'What quiz?' wrote Jai, clearly unable to keep up with
all these developments.

'A quiz where they're posting random photos
of people and places and food from both India
and Pakistan and asking people to guess which
country the photo is from.'

Jai sat up straight, wide awake now.

'That's phenomenal, Rusty!'

'Well. It's not *all* good, Jai. You also
have a few death threats from some people,
who kind of disapprove of you building these
bridges with "enemy" countries.'

'What?' spluttered Jai as he typed.

'Yep. But don't worry, I'm sure they'll
calm down as soon as they discover that you're
just a misguided schoolboy who plans to end the
Indo-Pak enmity, one Facebook post at a time.'

'I don't know if you're trying to help or
just having a good laugh at my expense.'

'I'm just telling you that I'm right behind
you while you try out these death-defying
escapades. Anyway, Ansh and Co. here are also
out to get you. You may as well die a martyr
by going ahead with your death-by-Facebook
plan instead.'

'You just wait, Rusty. I'll sort you out when I get back.'

'Kidding, just kidding! Listen, I've come up with some more captions for your campaign and mailed them to you. Now go check your Facebook page—it's absolutely insane!'

Jai couldn't believe his eyes when he clicked on his new Facebook page. There were messages from all over the world. Some from people he knew, but most were from complete strangers—writing in from across the globe. They had sent photographs of family and friends they had left behind. Or the homes they had abandoned. Others had sent in photographs for the quiz.

Jai sank into his chair, overwhelmed.

This *was* turning out to be quite a storm.

However, this one would have to wait. Because a storm was brewing closer to home when he flew back to India tomorrow. And today, he was hoping to meet Nabeel Said, when Inaya's match was done.

Touching Distance

Having defeated the team from Europe, the Curry Cruisers also managed to cut down the Saharan Superstars team from Africa, which qualified them for the finals of the Tape-ball League. Inaya and her teammates were over the moon—they hadn't, not even in their wildest dreams, imagined that they would make it so far. But now, they would play their toughest match—against the DownUnder Daredevils from Australasia—comprising players from Australia and New Zealand—who were the favourites and leaders of the league table.

News of the DownUnder Daredevils' captain Alison Warne's talent had reached every headline in the tape-ball circles. The coach assigned to the Curry Cruisers team had only one instruction for the girls: Warne was to be seen off early. Else, there was no hope of winning.

The Curry Cruisers lost the toss and were put in to bat first. They got off to quite a good start, but then their middle order collapsed, leading to a rather dismal total of 121 at the end of their innings.

The DownUnder Daredevils came in to bat, and from the outset, things did not go as per the Curry Cruisers' plan. Their skipper Warne opened the batting and scored a thumping 76, taking the DownUnder Daredevils to within touching distance of their target. But then, Warne's partner Emily Driver was dismissed, and two more wickets fell cheaply.

With 2 overs to go, the DownUnder Daredevils needed just 8 runs to win. Spectators started leaving the stands—the outcome was clear, there was nothing left in the match.

Shaheen, the captain of the Curry Cruisers threw the ball to Lubna, for the penultimate over.

'The ball is swinging well. Let's give it our best shot, Lubna,' she said, before running back to her fielding position.

Lubna nodded tacitly.

The first ball Lubna bowled was hit for a single by Doyle, giving Warne the strike. The next ball was struck well by Warne and would have fetched them 4 runs, was it not for some inspired fielding by Shaheen, who leapt sideways to stop it. Doyle and Warne still managed to take 2 runs.

5 runs needed. Ten balls in hand.

The third ball by Lubna was a beauty—Warne misread it completely, which almost cost her her wicket.

5 runs needed. Nine balls in hand.

Shaheen walked over to Lubna. 'Allow Warne an easy single so that Doyle is on strike,' she said.

The next ball by Lubna was slightly short of a length, and Warne nudged it into a gap in the field placement, getting a comfortable single. Warne was keen to come back for a second, but the fielding was too sharp for them to take the risk.

4 runs needed. Eight balls in hand.

The next ball was slower and Doyle misjudged it completely. She tried the pull shot, but without the pace, the ball ended up straight in a fielder's hands.

The Curry Cruisers leapt up in joy at the dismissal. Every little step counted.

The new batter in was Lily Daunt.

4 runs needed. Seven balls in hand.

Lubna took her run up and Daunt hit the ball for a single, just as Lubna had hoped. Warne didn't look keen to take the single because that would mean that Daunt would retain the strike, but Daunt had already started running.

It was the last over of the tournament and the DownUnder Daredevils needed just 3 runs to win.

Shaheen tossed the ball to Inaya, amidst an audible gasp from the crowd, who had all expected that the last over would be bowled by the Curry Cruisers' ace bowler, Alia.

'They don't know your style. I'm counting on that element of surprise,' said Shaheen, as Inaya looked at her, quite taken aback to have been given this huge responsibility. 'I've seen you bowl at the nets. You have a killer instinct. Go for it.'

She patted Inaya on the back and darted off.

Inaya took a deep breath. She looked around the field and signalled to fine leg and point to move up closer. She sent the fielder at sweeper cover further back.

Warne was not on strike, but with 6 balls to spare, the DownUnder Daredevils needed just 3 runs to win. All the batter had to do was get bat on ball, pinch a single and give the strike to Warne. But Inaya had other ideas in mind.

For the next 5 balls, Warne was reduced to a spectator, as Daunt couldn't connect with even a single one of Inaya's perfectly delivered, late-swinging yorkers.

There was just 1 ball to go. Inaya took a deep breath and took her run up. As the ball left her hand, she watched Daunt's bat connect with the ball, lifting it up and over her head. Inaya watched the ball's trajectory as it flew into the stands for 6 runs.

The DownUnder Daredevils had won. The stadium erupted in applause.

Inaya looked at the ground, crushed. She hadn't been able to save the match for her team. All their faith in her had been misplaced. Lubna came running up to her.

'Hey, that was some amazing bowling, Inaya!' she said, hugging her.

Shaheen joined them and patted Inaya on the back, 'Well played, Inaya!'

'Sorry, it wasn't good enough,' muttered Inaya, blinking back her tears.

Jai was disappointed for Inaya. But the silver lining was that the game was over—and he could now meet Nabeel Said. Hopefully.

His ears perked up when he heard the words 'Inaya Haider; she's from Pakistan' from behind him. He angled himself to listen.

Sitting right behind Jai watching the game was the coach for the women's cricket team for Middlesex and Simone Donnelly, the captain of the Chippy Champs side. The voice, which turned out to be Simone's continued, 'She's got a spark. She's wicked with the bat as well. I've played with her before.'

'Hmm . . . I'd like to meet her,' said the coach.

Twenty minutes had passed and there was still no sign of Inaya emerging from the dressing room. Jai assumed that she must be busy with her teammates and started collecting his things to leave. He needed to finish packing as there was a flight to be caught the next day.

'Hey Jai!' called an unfamiliar voice.

Jai turned around to see Nabeel Said standing with her arm around Inaya. He could barely believe his eyes.

'I hear that you're a gourmet,' said Nabeel. 'Are you free to come on a quick tour of my kitchens this afternoon? I'd love to get a pair of fresh eyes give me ideas about what I could be doing better.'

The DownUnder Daredevils may have won the match, but it was Jai who felt like he had just been handed the trophy.

He nodded, too overcome for words.

Filter Coffee

Heathrow Airport was busier than usual, which was a good thing because it was the perfect setting for Jai and Inaya's plan.

Since Toshi and Habib had yet to tell the rest of the family about them being siblings, Jai and Inaya had suggested that the best place to break the news would be in a public place, so that any reactions would be muted. Or at least, so they hoped.

After much deliberation, Heathrow Airport was the venue decided upon. The 'announcement' was to be made just before their respective flights took off. This would allow for an eight-hour long journey to allow Rajan, Arathi, Humaira and Irfan to come to terms with the revelation. The Puris were leaving London two days before the Haiders were, so Toshi and Jai had to do their bit first.

Rajan had first been in shock, then in denial. Arathi had almost fainted and it was only a strong filter coffee consumed in the safety of her own kitchen hours later that set her straight again.

Two days later, it was Habib and Inaya's turn. As soon as Habib broke the news, Humaira started chanting prayers under her breath and wouldn't listen to anything further that Habib had to say. Irfan simply pretended that he had urgent work calls to attend to and entertained no further discussion on the matter either.

Jai and Inaya had been in touch with each other over email and instant messaging, ever since Jai's return.

'How did the Big Announcement go? My parents may need aftershock therapy,' wrote Jai.

'Daadi has not stopped chanting prayers,' Inaya wrote back. 'And Abba is talking to imaginary people on the phone to deflect any further conversation on the topic.'

Jai grinned as he read this. 'Sounds familiar. Hey, thanks again for the Nabeel Said thing. She is such a star.'

'Glad it worked out. She seemed to like all your suggestions. You should follow-up on your café idea. You'd be okay at it.'

'Thanks,' typed Jai, not used to anything even slightly resembling a compliment from Inaya. 'You should keep going with tape-ball. And if you come to India, we'll go find Ghulan Joswami for you.'

Inaya burst out laughing as she read that.

'It's *Jhulan Goswami*, but thanks for the offer. Although judging by my family's reactions, the India trip may never happen.'

Deadlock

Rawalpindi, Pakistan

An awkwardness lingered in the air between Humaira, Habib and Irfan. There hadn't been a full-blown discussion of the matter—neither at the airport, nor on the flight, nor at home.

Inaya dreaded mealtimes. Dinner conversations were stilted and perfunctory, skimming the surface, skirting the periphery—as if Habib's revelation had made them strangers all of a sudden.

'How was school, Inaya?' asked Habib.

'It was good, Daada.'

Silence.

'Can I pass anyone the mutton curry?' asked Habib, looking at Humaira and Irfan.

'No, thank you,' said Humaira. 'I'm sure we can help ourselves.'

Irfan looked up from his plate.

'Excuse me, I have a work call,' he said, pushing his chair back.

'But it's so late . . . ' protested Habib.

'It's New York,' said Irfan abruptly and left the room.

Habib fell silent. Humaira stole a glance at him and it was then that Inaya knew that the showdown was imminent.

'I can't believe that you have lived your whole life as a lie, Habib,' she said, without looking up from her plate.

Habib looked at her, pained.

'I was six years old when I was adopted, Humaira. How is the time before that my *whole* life?'

'You could have still told me.'

'I thought I had lost everyone from my birth family, Humaira. Please understand I wasn't trying to deceive you. It was just very difficult to revisit that chapter of my life.'

'And now? What happens now that you've reopened this chapter?'

'Well, if you're okay with it, I'd love for us to go and visit my sister in India.'

Humaira looked too shocked to even dignify that suggestion with a response.

'What do you say, Humaira?' Habib reached out and touched Humaira's arm lightly.

Humaira turned to face Habib, an edge of steel in her voice. 'Do you want to know what I say, Habib? I say, over my dead body. I'm not going to India and neither are you. Do you not care at all that my grandfather was killed by Hindus in the Partition riots?'

'Humaira, I too lost my family in those riots. But I have reconnected with my sister after sixty years . . . '

'Yes—and she's Indian and Hindu . . . '

'Do you realize that you have been married for almost fifty years to someone who was born a Hindu, Humaira?' Habib replied softly.

'That . . . that is your fault. How was I to know? Oh, I pray I will not be punished for this.'

'I take the entire blame, Humaira. I will bear any sin that it carries, if that makes you feel any better.'

'It doesn't. And I still won't let you go to India.'

There was a moment's silence as Inaya watched both her grandparents continue to stare at their respective dinner plates. Deadlock, she thought. Then Habib spoke again.

'You've always spoken about visiting Chishti's dargah in Ajmer, Humaira. How about we go there too, when we visit India?'

Something stirred in Humaira. Chishti's dargah held a very special place in her life. Her mother and grandmother and almost every generation before had visited the Sufi saint's shrine to pay their respects. Perhaps this was a sign that her calling had come. Perhaps Habib needed to face his past. Perhaps she needed to face it too.

But she held her silence.

Later that night, after the whole family had retired for bed, Humaira took out her brown moleskin diary. She opened it and slid out the loose pages stacked inside. She looked at the sketches that she had collected over the years. Sketches that Habib had made in the dead of night, furiously drawing during his somnambulism. More than once, she had asked him about the sketches the next morning, and he had looked at them as if he had never seen them before. With her finger, Humaira traced around the circular scribble of the huddled figures and the line that cleaved across each sketch. The darkness and despair that they conveyed sent a shudder down her spine. For years, she had wondered about the deep pain that Habib held within himself—a trauma so torturous that he had kept it caged, but which reared its ugly head in his wakeful sleep. Humaira had never been able to understand where it came from. But now, it all fell into place.

Unforgotten

New Delhi, India

'But how come you never mentioned it, Ma? Not once?' asked Rajan.

Toshi took off her spectacles and looked at Rajan and Arathi. 'I didn't want to remember what had taken me a lifetime to forget,' she said simply. 'I don't expect you to understand.'

Arathi came over and sat down beside her mother-in-law. 'Ma, I've been thinking a great deal about this, but I can't fathom . . .'

Toshi looked at her with kindness, 'It's enough for me that you tried to see it my way, Arathi. We don't always have to agree about everything.'

'What I was going to say, Ma, is that I can't fathom how you went through life carrying so much heartache, all alone. I feel sad that you didn't think you could tell us about it. We might have helped lighten your burden of sorrow.'

Toshi smiled wistfully at her daughter-in-law, 'That load is the only thing that reminded me that I could still feel pain.

Leaving Tarlok all alone that day is the burden I carried every day of my life. It was my repentance. If I gave that away, I would have felt like I had failed him even further.'

You mustn't think that way, Ma . . . ' began Rajan.

'I can't imagine life without my sister,' cut in Arathi. 'If I don't call her at least twice a week, I feel like something is drastically wrong.'

'Twice a day is more like it,' said Rajan.

Arathi ignored his comment and carried on. 'Rajan, I think we should invite the Haiders to come and stay with us. One must spend quality time with one's family. Nothing is more important.'

Rajan's jaw dropped only a little more than Toshi's did.

The Envelope

A month or so passed without any further mention of an India trip. Habib had not pressed the matter, not wanting to upset Humaira. Irfan had immersed himself in his work so completely that he was barely seen by his family. He left for work at the crack of dawn and returned home late at night, leaving little time for any real discussion of the matter.

Early one morning, Habib went into the kitchen as usual and found Humaira there before him, reading the newspaper and sipping tea. His tea was on the tray along with the sports section of the newspaper that Humaira usually set aside for him, since Habib always said that all the other news tended to depress him. Lying by his newspaper was an envelope.

Habib sat down and took a sip of his tea. He reached for the letter opener and slit through the envelope. Inside it, were flight tickets to India. Four tickets, to be precise. Habib turned to Humaira, dumbfounded.

'I hope you're free in November, Habib?' said Humaira, casually looking up from her newspaper. 'There's an art gallery in Mumbai that is keen to exhibit your works. And I thought I may as well tag along, since you're so prone to aches and pains—you'll need someone to complain to. I've bought a ticket for Inaya as well because she seems rather desperate to meet this Jhulan Goswami. And as for Irfan, he needs to get out of that black hole of an office of his. Now it's your headache to arrange the visas.'

Habib was quiet for a few moments. Then he drew a slow, grateful breath.

'Thank you, Humaira,' he said.

Highway Robbers

New Delhi, India

The kitchen table in the Puri household was very full. The Haider family had arrived the day before and they were all sitting around the table, sipping tea while Toshi plied them with savoury and sweet snacks that she just wouldn't stop preparing. It was a heart-warming sight, all of them together. Habib was busy showing the Puris photographs of his adopted family.

'And that is my mother, Rukhsana, and my father, Javed—and that, is my grandmother, Arjumand,' he said, pointing them out.

'Oh, she's gorgeous! And what stunning jewellery she's wearing. Wait—hold on,' said Arathi, as Habib was about to turn the page in the album, 'That looks familiar doesn't it, Ma?'

She pointed to an ornament on Arjumand's forehead. Toshi came over and squinted at the photograph. Her breathing quickened.

'It cannot be,' she said softly.

'Are you saying what I think you're saying?' said Rajan, leaning in to have a closer look as well. 'That would be *such* a bizarre coincidence.'

'Well, let's find out,' said Arathi.

And as the Haiders watched in confusion, Arathi retrieved the paasa jhoomar and the diary. She carefully laid out the paasa jhoomar next to the photograph. It was an exact match.

'I believe this might have belonged to your grandmother,' said Arathi, looking at Habib.

'What! This is crazy. How do you have my great-great-grandmother's jewellery?' asked Inaya.

'We're highway robbers,' said Jai, with a straight face. 'We've got a stash of jewellery hidden behind our kitchen walls. Though some of it has been taken away by the mice that live there, for their children's weddings.'

'Oh, I had forgotten about the mice!' laughed Toshi.

'Are they always like this?' muttered Humaira to Habib. 'I thought you were bad enough, but your "real" family seems even crazier than your adopted one.'

Toshi came over to sit beside Humaira and handed her the piece of jewellery and the diary.

'This is rightfully yours,' she said. 'We found them both in a hidden alcove in our kitchen. And look, it says here that the diary belongs to Arjumand.'

Humaira stared at the diary in disbelief. She passed it to Habib, who slowly flipped through its yellowed pages and then read from it softly:

'17 August 1947. It is relentless, this madness that continues to possess us all. Javed tells me that we must leave our home, our

country and go. "Pack your things, Ammi," he said. What do I take? What do I leave behind? I will return to Musaafir Khaana, of that I am sure. That is what I told Ghanshyam when I left my things in his care. He says he will keep everything ready for Eid when the family arrives. Until then, may Allah keep my family safe . . . '

Habib looked up from the diary, stunned.

'So, is . . . is this Musaafir Khaana?' he asked. 'My Daadi couldn't stop talking about it right up until the very end.'

'Well, I believe Musaafir Khaana was converted into four apartments sometime in the 1950s,' said Rajan. 'So, I guess we're sitting in one quarter of it.'

'She would always say that she would come back to Musaafir Khaana . . . ' Habib continued in a quiet reverie.

'And in a way she has,' said Humaira, gently placing her hand on Habib's. 'Along with us.'

'Is it all right if I take a photograph of the four of you, I mean the Haider family, with this diary and jewellery?' asked Jai.

'Most certainly,' said Humaira. 'As long as we have another photograph after that with all of us, the whole family, in it.'

Seeing Toshi's eyes well up on hearing this, Arathi gave her a quick hug.

'I hate to admit I was wrong, but I was, Ma,' she whispered. 'I cannot even imagine why I ever had a problem sitting at the same table as them! They're so incredibly nice.'

'Can everyone please stop looking so weepy?' said Jai, noticing the expressions of his grandmother, mother, Humaira and Habib. 'I have photographs to take.'

'Are you still doing that Peace-ing It Together thing, by the way?' asked Inaya.

Jai nodded, bracing himself for her usual withering derision of his ideas. 'It's not such a waste of time as you consider it. We've had a lot of responses from people across the world and—'

'I actually think it's a really good idea,' Inaya cut in.

Now it is was Jai's turn to gape.

'In fact, I'm going to request Nabeel Said to help us with spreading the word for Peace-ing It Together. Perhaps we can have an Indo-Pak Food Week at her cafés? And on her website, people could post photographs of food that is eaten on both sides of the border?'

'That's great,' said Jai, beaming. 'And, by the way, my parents have gotten us tickets to watch Ghulan Joswami's match in Mumbai.'

'It's *Jhulan Goswami!* For the hundredth time!' laughed Inaya, but her eyes shone with delighted anticipation.

'There's no guarantee that she'll meet us, but we can try,' said Jai, not wanting to raise Inaya's expectations too high, in case it didn't work out. Especially since he had no idea how he was going to go about this whole exercise in the first place. Reaching Mumbai and going to watch her match was his grand plan so far.

'And after Habib's art show in Mumbai, we will all go to Ajmer,' said Toshi. 'To Chishti's dargah.'

'What's that?' asked Inaya.

Toshi smiled at her. 'Chishti was a Sufi saint, Inaya. He was born in Iran, but he chose Ajmer as his home—

so that's where his shrine is. People called him Khwaja Gharib Nawaz, meaning "patron saint of the poor". But even the richest came to him. Emperor Akbar would often walk from Agra to Ajmer to seek his blessings and offer thanks. I cannot wait to visit with all of you. I have so many thanks to offer.'

She took Humaira's and Habib's hands and held them to her eyes, just as her father would do with Tarlok and her as children.

Life had come full circle.

Travel Companions

Mumbai, India

Habib had booked them all into one of the finest five star hotels in the city and wouldn't listen to Rajan and Arathi's protests about wanting to pay for their rooms themselves.

'It's the least I can do for my sister, after all these years,' he said.

'But you're . . . ' Rajan had started to say but then stopped himself from finishing the sentence. *A guest in our country.*

Inaya couldn't wait to attend the cricket match—and perhaps get the chance to meet her hero, Jhulan. It was a day-night game, and she had been ready a good hour before they were supposed to leave, waiting restlessly in the hotel lobby for Jai and the rest.

Twenty long minutes later, everyone was finally in the lobby. Humaira, Irfan and Inaya were wearing the Pakistan cricket team's green T-shirts, while Jai, Rajan and Arathi were in the Indian team's blue ones. Toshi and Habib were the only two not wearing the team T-shirts.

'Aren't you coming, Badi Ma?' asked Jai.

Toshi shook her head and smiled, 'While all of you watch the match, I thought I'd take Loki—I mean Habib—to meet some of our cousins. He hasn't seen them since he was six. And then, when the match is over, we'll meet you back at the hotel for dinner.'

'If he complains too much about aches and pains, just ignore him, Toshi Aapa,' said Humaira.

'Good idea, Humaira. I'll take my hearing aid off, if he starts,' laughed Toshi. 'Now go, all of you—the car is waiting—enjoy the match.'

'And say hello to Jhulan for me,' added Habib, ruffling Inaya's curly hair.

The match was completely enrapturing for Inaya. She had never watched a women's cricket game live before—and to watch Jhulan Goswami play right before her eyes, that too against Australia, was simply beyond anything she could imagine.

Jhulan was on fire. She managed to get four quick wickets and keep the Aussie scoring under control. At the end of the Aussie innings, Inaya waited breathlessly by the side of the steps, as the players returned to the pavilion for their break. As Jhulan passed by her, Inaya desperately wanted to say something but found herself tongue-tied.

Jai uncharacteristically jumped into the fray, 'Er, Jhulan!' he shouted. 'Your biggest fan from Pakistan is here and wants to say hello.'

Jhulan Goswami looked up at Jai. Jai pointed to Inaya. Jhulan sportingly ran back to shake Inaya's hand.

'Good to meet you. Thanks for coming all the way to watch me.'

'She's an amazing tape-ball cricket player herself,' added Jai, since Inaya was still in a dumbfounded state. 'Her name is Inaya Haider. She was runner-up in the tape-ball league match in the UK.'

'Fabulous!' said Jhulan. 'Good luck, Inaya. Keep playing.'

Inaya looked like she might faint with happiness. Jai was more relieved than anything else that his Jhulan problem had been sorted for now.

Sitting beside them, Humaira, Irfan, Rajan and Arathi who had started out rather awkwardly, were all getting on quite famously now, animatedly discussing Bollywood films, Pakistani dramas, cricket and food—not necessarily in that order.

'Okay, so it's settled then. You give us Coke Studio, we give you Katrina Kaif,' said Arathi.

Irfan pretended to sign an imaginary document, which he then handed to Arathi with an exaggerated flourish.

'It's a deal,' he said.

'Oh please—that sounds like a very unfair trade,' protested Rajan. 'Why don't you take one of our strapping heroes instead?'

Humaira smiled, listening to their banter. 'I'm so glad you made the time to get away from work, Irfan,' she said.

'Oh, is he a workaholic as well?' asked Arathi. 'It must be a family trait then.'

'I'm not a workaholic,' declared Rajan and Irfan, almost in unison, throwing up their hands.

Humaira and Arathi exchanged a look and burst out laughing.

Meanwhile, Habib and Toshi took a cab back to their hotel, exhausted but happy after their day spent together, visiting their cousins. As the taxi drew up outside the hotel, Toshi pointed to the Gateway of India framed against the inky sea and sky.

'Do you remember we used to buy peanuts from that vendor here?' she asked, her eyes shining as if she were ten again. 'How much we'd laugh when he called peanuts "timepass"—we'd never heard that before.'

Habib laughed.

'Those were good days, Toshi di. And you're looking as happy as if you're expecting that he will still be here.'

'You never know—perhaps his son or daughter could be here? Now I can believe that almost anything is possible. I'll buy us some peanuts for old time's sake and be back in two minutes.'

'Okay, I'll book us a table at the restaurant in the meanwhile,' said Habib. 'Hopefully, their match should be done soon?'

Toshi nodded and wandered off in search of the peanut vendor. She inhaled the warm sea breeze laden with happy childhood memories. She couldn't find the peanut vendor she was looking for, but she did get the peanuts. She tried one and shut her eyes happily as a wave of nostalgia washed over her.

Toshi looked up to the sky. There were an uncommon number of crows flying over the red domes of the hotel. Biji always said that crows brought messages from loved ones who had died. Perhaps Biji and Papaji were sending Tarlok and her a message today, she thought with a smile.

Her thoughts were interrupted by the sound of fireworks. Toshi turned around. The sound seemed to be coming from the hotel—a wedding celebration, possibly. It was November after all, the season for weddings, and the concierge had mentioned that there was to be a 'big fat Indian wedding' that night.

Then she heard it again. This sound was definitely not fireworks. It was more like the crackle of machine-gun fire.

Tarlok.

The packet of peanuts fell from her hand. The people around her started running helter-skelter. The panic was palpable, descending on them like a shroud.

'Terrorist attack!' shouted someone.

'Run!' shouted another man. He grabbed his young daughter by the hand, and as he did so, her doll fell to the ground. Within seconds, it was mangled under the feet of the stampeding crowd.

Toshi felt emptied to the pit of her stomach. It was as if the same nightmare born of hatred was replaying itself. Toshi's doll, Nanhi, lying on the ground trampled underfoot by a frenzied mob. Toshi could almost see her six-year-old brother standing amidst the chaos, alone. Except, this time, she wasn't going to let him be alone.

She started running towards the hotel, as fast as her arthritic legs would carry her.

'Don't go that way,' shouted a well-meaning vendor, who was hurriedly collecting his wares and fleeing the scene.

Toshi took no heed. Whatever this was, this time around she would not leave Tarlok's side. She rushed through the hotel lobby and towards the restaurant where Tarlok had headed to make the booking. The smell of gunpowder hung ominously in the air.

As she entered the restaurant, from the corner of her eye, Toshi saw a man being gunned down. She stopped—rooted to the spot in a stunned stupor. A familiar terror uncoiled like a sludge to pulse through her veins, as the man collapsed in a pool of blood. Slowly, Toshi forced herself to turn around to look at him.

What struck her first was that it wasn't Tarlok. What struck her next was that the man's eyes were wide open, his mouth forming an oval as if he had been abruptly cut off mid-sentence. The blood from his temple dripped in a steadily increasing pattern on to the napkin that was still on his lap. Like a tap that hadn't been fully shut off. Around him were bodies of other people. Women, men. Just stacked on top of each other in a tangle of limbs.

The image of a train went through Toshi's head. The blood-drenched platform at Rawalpindi when she was ten. That was what this reminded her of. She recoiled from that memory, as if someone had physically struck her in the face. Her breath became laboured. She could hear her heartbeat pound against her eardrum. But one thought eclipsed everything else.

Tarlok.

She had to find Tarlok. Getting down on her hands and knees, Toshi made her way behind the tables, crawling slowly through the room, pushing past lifeless bodies, her eyes searching for Tarlok. There was the sound of gunshots again. The gunmen were in the room. Toshi shut her eyes and lay flat on her stomach, not knowing where or whom the shots would hit. And then, as she opened her eyes, she spotted Tarlok sitting at the far end of the room. Her spirits soared. Tarlok was alive and safe. He saw her too and smiled. Toshi waited for the gunshots to subside, and then she quietly crawled towards her brother and sat beside him, careful not to make a sound.

It was then that she noticed the crimson crater in the side of his stomach, which left his insides hanging out.

Toshi's heart seemed to stop beating. Instinctively, she reached for the tablecloth to stem the blood flow. And it was that movement that attracted the attention of the gunman.

As best as she could, Toshi wrapped the tablecloth around her brother's wound. Which was when the first bullet hit her leg. She reached for Tarlok's hand and that was when the second bullet hit her chest.

Toshi feebly took her brother's hand and touched it to her eyes.

Just as their father would do.

Holding on to Tarlok's hand, Toshi's mind drifted far away to a leafy gully in Rawalpindi. Only this time, she didn't leave his side.

Unseen

Humaira didn't shed a single tear. All she did was pray. And when she finally spoke, all she said was that she wanted Habib to be buried not in Rawalpindi, but near the Ajmer Sharif Dargah. Irfan looked at his mother in shock. But her jaw was set firm.

'It's what Habib would have wanted,' she said with quiet resolve.

As the family prepared to leave for Ajmer, Inaya picked up her grandfather's coat and held it close. She sat there in silence, like one would with an old, familiar friend, where no conversation was necessary. She dug her hands into the large pockets, trying to feel the warmth and safety of her grandfather's embrace, one last time. Her fingers came across something hard in one of the pockets. She took the object out—it was the oval, olive-coloured pebble that her grandfather always carried with him.

'Why do you carry this around with you, Daada?' Inaya had once asked him.

Habib had smiled at Inaya and sat her down, holding the quartz pebble out for her in his palm.

'Do you know how long this pebble has been around, Inaya?'

'Since the time you were a little boy?'

'Even longer. A few hundred million years perhaps. Inside it is folded a story of survival that we cannot even imagine. It's my rock of hope,' he had said.

If only she could hear his voice again. Just one more time. Just to say goodbye even. Inaya's cheeks were wet with the tears that quietly rolled down.

She slipped the pebble into her own pocket. His rock of hope would be hers now. For always.

Wrapped in centuries of wondrous reverence, the Ajmer Sharif Dargah of Khwaja Moinuddin Chishti came into view.

Holding the urn of his grandmother's ashes close to his heart, Jai followed the slow shuffle of hundreds of feet, as they made their way towards the Sufi saint's final resting place. His attention was drawn by a heady fragrance and he turned to see the bathing ritual of the tomb being carried out by its custodians, the *khadims,* as they doused the *mazaar* with rosewater infused with saffron and sandalwood. Lamps with ghee were lit in the four corner niches, peacock feathers were used to sweep the floor. Fresh flowers and exquisitely embroidered covers were laid on the tomb. It was the strangest combination of Hindu and Muslim customs, and yet, somehow, it seemed just right. Jai felt a stirring in the stillness; a cool breeze that caressed his moist forehead.

Almost like Badi Ma would. He blinked back his tears and held the urn closer.

A few paces behind them, Inaya quietly sidled up to Humaira and held her hand. She looked around her and saw people in deep meditation, some on a prayer mat facing Mecca, others chanting Vedic scriptures, turbaned Sikhs in silent contemplation.

'Do you think Allah is here Daadi, along with all the other gods that these people are praying to?' she asked.

Humaira looked at her granddaughter's earnest face searching for answers.

'I don't know, my kishmish. I have never seen Allah. I don't know if anyone has seen their gods. But Gharib Nawaz reaches the divine without any of these imaginary boundaries. He will make sure that Habib is in good hands,' she replied, with moist eyes. 'And Toshi Aapa too.'

Inaya tightened her clutch around the little pebble in her pocket and swallowed the lump in her throat.

2012

'I've tried to become someone
else for a while, only to discover
that he, too, was me.'
—*Stephen Dunn,* Here and Now: Poems

Pitching It Right

In a leafy gully in Rawalpindi, where a young girl once played pithoo with her brother, another young girl played tape-ball cricket, sixty-odd years later.

The month she turned nineteen, Inaya Haider made her debut in Pakistan's women's cricket team, opening their batting. Watching his daughter walk out on to the pitch, Irfan fought back his tears of joy. Standing beside him, Humaira wept copiously.

In that very match, Inaya scored her maiden fifty. As the stadium erupted into thunderous applause, Inaya reached into her pocket, took out an olive green oval pebble, held it in her outstretched arm and gave the sky a huge smile. From behind the clouds, she could almost see her mother and grandfather smile back at her.

Meanwhile, eighteen-year-old Jai Puri started an online cooking channel, which he named 'Toshi's Kitchen'. It gained quite a fan following and was even endorsed by Nabeel Said, thanks to a little help from Inaya.

Despite his apathy for cricket, Jai now knows a thing or two about the game, never misses a single match that Inaya plays in—and wildly cheers her on.

However, if it is an India-Pakistan match, things are different. Then Jai roots for India. And after the match, Inaya and he have heated debates about which team deserved to win.

It is full-blown war. However, it always abides by the spirit of the sport.

After all, the sports pitch is perhaps the only place where this war should happen. Between the two nations, across the line.

epilogue

'We leave something of ourselves behind when we leave a place.
We stay there, even though we go away. And there are things
in us that we can find again only by going back.'

—*Pascal Mercier,* Night Train to Lisbon

What Did I Miss?

Boasting original ownership by Napolean III's favourite chef, the Gaslight was *the* place to be seen at, in London's 1960s. Which, of course, was why Antonia Radcliffe had chosen the restaurant for the luncheon with Claire and Pauline. To which, she would, of course, arrive fashionably late.

A waiter materialized with a platter of hors d'oeuvres, which he set down in front of the two elegant ladies seated across each other, at a table for three. Deeply engrossed in conversation, Claire and Pauline barely noticed its arrival.

'Do you honestly think we should tell Antonia about that ghastly poem?' asked Claire. Her words seemed to imply that they shouldn't mention it, although her smug expression suggested entirely the opposite.

'Well, if it's in the papers and it's by W.H. Auden, she's bound to find out about it,' said Pauline. 'Is it really all that bad?'

225

'Goodness, yes. It shows Cyril in the most unflattering light. Have a look for yourself—especially the last few lines.'

Claire reached into her handbag and handed a newspaper to Pauline. The words 'Partition: A Poem by W.H. Auden' caught her eye. Pauline began to read it, at first in silence, and then, murmuring the last few lines aloud, as if to convince herself that this had actually appeared in print.

> *The weather was frightfully hot,*
> *And a bout of dysentery kept him constantly on the trot,*
> *But in seven weeks it was done, the frontiers decided,*
> *A continent for better or worse divided.*
> *The next day he sailed for England, where he quickly forgot*
> *The case, as a good lawyer must. Return he would not,*
> *Afraid, as he told his Club, that he might get shot.*

'Oh dear, this *is* quite harsh. But it was hardly like Cyril drew that line of his own choosing,' said Pauline. 'Antonia says that he doesn't want to be reminded of it at all. Says he burnt all the papers connected with it. And even returned his fee of £3000.'

Claire looked over her shoulder and dropped her voice to the breathy whisper of confidences, 'Well, some would say that Cyril was rewarded handsomely enough upon his return from India. I mean, to be made a Law Lord without ever having been a Judge!' Claire raised a suggestive eyebrow, indicating just how out of turn that was. 'And then, a few months later, he was suddenly a Baron! Don't you remember how chuffed Antonia was at becoming Lady Radcliffe, flaunting it in our faces at every chance?'

'Oh, come now, Claire. I think we're being a little unkind here,' said Pauline. 'If anything, it was that crooked Dickie Mountbatten and his lust for laurels that forced Cyril's hand. And *he* gained far more from the whole exercise than poor Cyril did.'

'I guess you're right, Pauline,' conceded Claire, sipping her Pimm's. 'In any case, it was the fault of the squabbling Indian and Pakistani governments. Appallingly poor governance—how else could a million people die just by the drawing of a line?'

Pauline nodded distractedly, as she tried to catch a waiter's attention for more pressing matters. Her White Lady wasn't quite chilled enough.

Just then, Antonia Radcliffe breezed into the restaurant in her perfumed paisley, pashmina and pearls.

'I'm so sorry to keep you waiting, darlings,' she gushed. 'Tell me, what did I miss?'

Ever so discreetly, Claire pushed the newspaper closer to Antonia's chair, so that she might happen to spot it.

Erasure

The man looked up from the maps he had been poring over. His hands were clammy, partly from the heat but mostly from the enormity of the task he had been assigned. He mopped the sweat off his brow. Then, Cyril Radcliffe picked up his pen, drew a deep breath—and started to write.

> *Dear Dickie,*
>
> *I regret to inform you that I cannot draw this line—especially not in the manner and time frame that you have asked. My conscience will not allow it. Not even for Crown or country. Because, before all else, I am answerable to myself.*
>
> *Yours truly,*
> *Cyril Radcliffe*

He set the pen down. There. The deed was done.

He felt lighter. Afloat almost.

'Cyril, it's time for supper,' said Antonia, as she gently shook him awake.

Radcliffe opened his eyes, now almost completely clouded with cataracts, to see his wife standing next to his armchair. He sat up with a start.

'Is everything all right, dear?' Antonia asked.

Radcliffe nodded absently. He slowly stood up and shuffled to the window.

The sun was setting. There was nothing half-hearted about the autumn. A luminous sapphire sky framed a canopy of scarlet leaves. Radcliffe watched a solitary leaf languidly drift and finally settle on the ground, adding to the burgundy patchwork quilt that covered the earth. It would be winter soon. Followed by spring. The colours of nature erasing what was written before.

Cyril Radcliffe stood at the window, looking out into the fading light of dusk.

If only all lines could be erased.

If only.

Author's Note

This book probably started writing itself many years ago, owing to an unspoken conversation. One that I wish I'd had but didn't.

I was about ten years old, and as we always did over the school holidays, my parents, my brother and I journeyed from Kolkata to my grandparents' farm in a little village in north India. At the time, I didn't know that my grandparents had spent their childhood and youth in Rawalpindi, Lahore and Sargodha. I didn't know that they had arrived in New Delhi as refugees in 1947, alongside millions of others, with just the clothes on their back, having lost loved ones in an upheaval so deeply traumatic that it never found mention in our conversations. Except, perhaps, that one time—had I stayed and spoken.

Afternoons at the farm were sweltering—too hot for tractor rides or skimming stones on the canal or splashing around in the tube well, which is what my brother and I would usually spend the rest of the day doing. So, our afternoon ritual was to laze around on the divan in my grandfather's study, with the bamboo blinds lowered and the air-cooler blowing khus-khus scented breeze our way. Some days, my grandfather would ask us to select a book from his huge collection of Urdu novels and poetry, and then he would read to us. Having grown up in Rawalpindi, he was fluent in Urdu but couldn't read Hindi. I couldn't read Urdu but could understand it enough to get by, so this arrangement worked pretty well for me; although, my brother, who was younger, would usually wander off to play with our cook's son instead.

One afternoon, I selected a book and handed it to my grandfather. He looked at it, hesitated ever so slightly, and then announced its name *Phundne*, which meant 'tassels', he said. He told me it was a collection of short stories by Saadat Hasan Manto—and the story he chose to read to me was called *Toba Tek Singh*.

By way of backdrop, my grandfather explained that this story was set in a lunatic asylum, a few years after the Partition. It began with the governments of Pakistan and India having decided to swap their lunatics along religious lines, just as they had done with the rest of their people—so that all Hindus, Sikhs and Muslims ended up on the 'right' side of the border. I remember thinking this a rather silly plotline, but there was little else to do, so I listened. Manto's dark satire as to who then were the *real* lunatics was lost on me, of course.

I can still recall my grandfather's voice, assuming different intonations as he read. He had me in splits as he muttered the well-known rant of the story's protagonist: '*Upar di gur gur di annexe di be dhiyana di mung di daal of di Pakistan and Hindustan of di durr phitey munh.*' I had no clue of its context, but it sounded nonsensically amusing. Between peals of laughter, I looked up to notice that my grandfather had stopped reading. He sat slumped forward, his hands covering his face, his shoulders convulsing as he sobbed.

I had never seen my grandfather cry before—or ever after—but that day, my otherwise fearless grandfather, who had braved lathi charges and prison in the fight for independence, wept. At a loss for what to do, I went to call my grandmother. In stunned silence, I watched her comforting him as if he were a little child, murmuring '*Chhado*, *mitti pao*'—let it go, bury it. And then I quietly left the room. Later that evening, I remember hiding that book behind all his other books, so I would never happen to take it out again. And never have to see my grandfather cry.

What I didn't do was ever ask him what caused those tears. The regret still leaves me feeling empty.

As the years went by, my grandparents shared countless anecdotes about their early days in undivided India. The pranks they would get up to with their friends at school and the trouble it got them into with their teachers and parents. The uncooked legs of lamb that they would sneak into the kitchen garden to be slow-roasted overnight in the tandoor pit, without my strictly vegetarian great-grandmother's knowledge. The street plays they would stage to protest against British rule. Their stories were peppered with fond anecdotes of their neighbours—Hindus, Muslims, Sikhs, Parsis—who had lived next door for generations. I would listen, enraptured, piecing together the fragments in my head, imagining the people and places that once made up their world.

Yet, what they never spoke about was the events surrounding the Partition itself. Perhaps it was just too painful to reopen the wounds. Perhaps, as refugees, grief was a luxury they could ill afford. Or perhaps, gaining independence had demanded centre stage instead. I sometimes wonder, on each Independence Day, did they also quietly mourn who and what they'd lost in the aftermath?

This book, then, is my attempted tribute to a generation of quiet heroes on either side of the border, who silently bore the brunt of a cataclysmic rupture in their lives. A generation that wordlessly erased its past and gave their all to building our future. And most strikingly, a generation who, despite everything they had been through, harboured no malice. Maybe because they had seen first-hand that there were no 'good' and 'bad' people. That, alternatively, the aggressors had also been the victims. That an eye for an eye did indeed make us blind, and easier to manipulate by those whom it suited.

In these tumultuous times, as the world gets alarmingly less tolerant, we might do well to take a leaf from their book—to seek out what we share rather than what divides us and not hand history the chance to repeat itself.

I'd like to think that perhaps this story chose me to allow me a chance to make amends, in some small way, for not finding the words, when I should have.

I hope these words do make a difference to someone, somewhere.

Bibliography

✠ Pratchett, Terry. *A Hat Full of Sky*. London: Corgi Childrens, 2005.

✠ Saint-Exupéry, Antoine de. *The Little Prince*. San Diego: Harcourt, Inc., 2000.

✠ Pratchett, Terry. *Sourcery*. New York City: Harper, 2008.

✠ Turow, Scott. *Ordinary Heroes*. New York City: Warner Books, 2005.

✠ Dunn, Stephen. *Here and Now: Poems*, New York: W.W. Norton & Company, 2011

✠ Mercier, Pascal. *Night Train to Lisbon*, trans. Barbara Harshav, 2007

✠ United Nations High Commissioner for Refugees (UNHCR). 'The State of The World's Refugees 2000: Fifty Years of Humanitarian Action'. Last accessed 11 October 2019. https://www.unhcr.org/3ebf9bab0.pdf.

Acknowledgements

I have no idea why a particular story chooses us. Or why it gets told when it does. I've come to believe that long before a story is born, the universe earmarks the people who will be involved in its telling; their paths then cross by exquisite design—and the pieces serendipitously fall into place when the stars align.

If you indulge my seemingly far-fetched drift, it doesn't take a village—it takes a galaxy (with a publisher in it) to raise a story. And an author who shows up to write, day after day—hoping, against all odds, that the galaxy will also do its bit.

Luckily for me, the galaxy obliged. I have been ever so fortunate to cross paths with some incredibly special people who helped shape this book along the way. For which, I owe many grateful thanks.

To Pervin and Sean Mahoney, for their invaluable inputs and generous friendship. I must have done something truly wonderful to deserve having them in my corner.

To the absolutely phenomenal team at Penguin Random House India—Sohini Mitra, Smit Zaveri, Piya Kapur,

Aditi Batra—for their belief in my stories and for taking my words to a better place, always. It has been such a joy to work with you.

To Devangana Dash. Thanks to her amazing talent, I hope this book is judged by its cover.

To Rajan Navani, Vikram Sathaye, Asma Said Khan (my inspiration for Nabeel Said's character), Aliya Suleman, Sangeeta Datta, Chintan Girish Modi, Baela Raza Jamil, Ting Wang, Sunaina Shivpuri, Avi Gulati, Deepak Melwani, Dr Adwaita Menon (ace tape-ball cricket consultant), Jyotsna Gadi, Noreen Kazim and Bodhijit Ray—for their unhesitating and enthusiastic support in finding a wider reach for this little book.

To all the contributors to The Partition Museum in Amritsar, The 1947 Partition Project at Stanford University and The Oral History Project—The Citizens Archive of Pakistan; and the lovely staff at the British Library.

To my parents and my brother, Nishchae, for their boundless duas that guide my hand to write.

To Nandana and Vrinda, for reading every single draft and coming up with uncannily insightful plot points. And more than anything else, for gifting me with precious memories of our shared writing adventures.

To Vivek, for always believing, even when I floundered, and making it all possible.

Thank you everyone. For helping me tell a story that is very close to my heart.

Red Card
Kautuk Srivastava

One team. One year. Everything to lose.

When Rishabh Bala reaches the tenth standard, life takes a turn for the complicated. The bewildered boy feels the pressure of the looming board exams and finds himself hopelessly and hormonally in love. But what he yearns for most is victory on the field: at least one trophy with his beloved school football team.

Set in the suburban Thane of 2006, here is a coming-of-age story that runs unique as it does familiar. Hopscotching from distracted classrooms and tired tutorials to triumphs and tragedies on muddy grounds, this is the journey of Rishabh and his friends from peak puberty to the cusp of manhood.

READ MORE IN PENGUIN

Toppers
Aayush

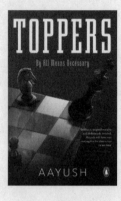

How far will you go to be the best?

Manipulation and lies reign supreme at the elite school of Woodsville. The race for the coveted spot of head scholar sees stakes being raised and sides taken as the student body turns into a pawn in a vicious game played by Woodsville's toppers: a charismatic royal, a calculating damsel in distress, the school star who had it all, a topper who cannot lose, a soft-spoken boy tired of living in the shadows and an unstoppable child prodigy.

Witness an intense battle of wills where the toppers overcome their demons only to unleash those lying in wait within others. Chaos and mayhem become their playthings as the facades slowly begin to crumble. But in their fight to be the best, they forget one thing . . . there's always someone better.

Fast-paced, riveting and intense, *Toppers* is the edge-of-the-seat dramatic thriller you've been waiting for all year.

'Armed with ambition and a politics that is rarely found in the genre, the book invents a new space for itself' *Firstpost*

READ MORE IN PENGUIN

Asmara's Summer
Andaleeb Wajid

'For a month, I'm going to be living a lie.'

Smart, sassy, popular, Asmara has a secret that could absolutely destroy her street cred in college: her grandparents live on Tannery Road, a conservative, not-so-posh part of town filled with claustrophobic houses and fashion disasters. So imagine her despair when she finds out that she has to spend her entire summer vacation there . . . possibly without Internet!

Funny, filmy and wildly entertaining, *Asmara's Summer* will send you into fits of giggles and tug at your heartstrings at the same time.